Hold Me, Babe

O'Neil De Noux

© 2016 O'Neil De Noux

Hold Me, Babe

For Joseph Hartlaub
thanks for the inspiration

Cover Art © 2016 O'Neil De Noux

Hold Me, Babe is a work of fiction. The incidents and characters described herein are a product of the author's imagination and are used fictitiously. Any resemblance to actual persons living or dead, business establishments, events, or locales is entirely coincidental. All rights reserved. No portion of this book may be reproduced by any means, electronic, mechanical, or otherwise, without the written permission of the copyright holder.
Author Web Site: http://www.oneildenoux.net
Twitter: ONeilDeNoux

Hold Me, Babe is as historically accurate as I could make it, but it is a novel, a work of fiction. If mistakes of fact were made from errors in research, by omission or design, well, it happens. We know the hula hoop did not come around until 1958 – Dx

Published by
Big Kiss Productions
New Orleans
First Printing 2016

THIS IS NEW ORLEANS
1951

THE CLIENT WAS late, so I stepped over to my office windows to look out at Barracks Street, see what the hell was happening in the neighborhood. Dark already, harsh shadows from streetlights filtered through the oaks and magnolias of Cabrini Park across the street, and a large black and white cat moved along the top of the playground's brick wall. He had a huge head, like a small football. He was one of the resident tom cats here.

Two evenings ago I saw this guy and an orange tabby go at it. Lot of howling, posturing, snarling but no actual combat. Reminded me of the Italian soldiers I met during the war. Prisoners, they argued a lot, howled, postured, made obscene gestures but no one ever threw a punch. I've heard if two tom cats occupied the same territory, one automatically took the day shift, the other took nights so they didn't clash and since most of the females were night gals, this one must have won the argument.

The night shift cat stopped and crouched, watching the trees in the playground. Was that a bird squawking? Yep. A mockingbird swooped from the nearest magnolia tree, dove at the cat who flattened itself but didn't move. I thought the mockingbird would take the hint. This was no kitten. Damn mockingbird must have had a nest in the tree because the sucker had swooped at me yesterday and all I did was park my car on this side of the street.

The mockingbird came back, squawking to give itself away. Bird brain. As it dove for the cat, the feline showed why it was a top predator and leapt up, swatted the bird in mid-flight, came down on the banquette – what we call

Hold Me, Babe

sidewalks here in New Orleans. The bird flapped away, minus a passel of feathers. The cat licked its paw as a long white Cadillac pulled up to park behind my Ford, blocking my view of the wildlife drama.

A thick fellow in a prim blue chauffeur's uniform stepped out of the Caddy, a bulky car, lot of chrome and low-bodied. Looked like a new '51 model. He wore a chauffeur's cap, tall black boots and looked at my building and I wondered if someone passed an onion under his nose. He shrugged and headed for the front door, which I'd left unlocked.

I spied a shadow beyond the frosted glass of my office door. It opened and the chauffeur peeked in, asked, "You the detective?"

"Detective?" I looked around furtively for a moment, looked back and his eyes had narrowed. I had to work on my greeting. I tried a smile. "Yes. I'm Lucien Caye."

He crossed the room, leaving the door open behind him, glancing at the wall of windows on his left that faced Barracks Street where the cat and bird had been jousting. His gaze moved to the other side of the room to the open kitchen and door to the bathroom.

I moved back to my oversized desk, leaned against it as he arrived. He was my height, six feet, the cap adding a couple inches and he outweighed my lean frame. His face was pock-marked from adolescent acne, but he hadn't been an adolescent for a good thirty years. He reached into his jacket and pulled out a white envelope, nodded for me to take it. Unsealed, the envelope was of fine cream-colored stationery. I opened it, found a folded letter with a check inside. The stationery heading, in fine copperplate, read:

Brienne
22 Audubon Place
New Orleans, Louisiana

The letter was typed, addressed to me:

Dear Mr. Caye:
At your earliest convenience, please come to 22 Audubon Place where you will be engaged to investigate a most serious matter. The enclosed check is a down payment for your services. You may advise the messenger who brought this letter the date and time of your expected arrival so we may inform the guard at the entrance to our community to admit you.

Sincerely,
Angél Brienne

PS: Show this letter to the guard when you come.

I held the stationery up to the light and saw the watermark showing it was made from 100% linen fibers. I caught a whiff of perfume. It wasn't the chauffeur. I looked at the check and tried not to let out a whistle.

I looked back at the man's beady eyes and said, "Monday morning? Eleven a.m.?" I figured rich types didn't get up too early.

He nodded, turned and crossed the room, closed the door. I watched the Caddy pull away. No cat or mockingbird out there now. I looked back at the check and it was still for a $1,000. *Damn*. It's good I only handle 'most serious matters'. I pressed the letter against my nose and recognized the scent. My Sin.

Damn. A cool grand.

And this wasn't the client I was expecting. The man who called me a couple hours ago said his name was Couralt or Courant.

The office door opened again and Jeannie came in, a pillow in hand.

"Why are you in your pajamas, Sweetie?"

"It's almost time." Her eyes grew wide.

"Time for what?"

She let out a sigh, shaking her head as she crossed the long room to my desk and pointed up at the electric clock on the far wall.

"Ella and the Pirates."

"We have time."

She put a hand on her hip. "We have to make popcorn."

It's been nearly a year since Jeannie's mother dropped her off at my doorstep with a suitcase and a birth certificate naming me the father of this dark haired girl with eyes identical to my Mediterranean brown eyes. I still got goose bumps, almost daily, discovering something about Jeannie that's so much like me. She'll be eight in a few weeks. Still a little girl, thankfully.

A movement at the office door caught my eye as a small man in a rumpled brown suit and carrying a tan portfolio peeked in.

"Mr. Caye?"

I waved him in.

"I am Edward Courant. We spoke on the phone." He was about five-five, with Albert Einstein white hair and eyebrows like fat caterpillars, yet his eyes were bright and he smiled at Jeannie as I asked her to go upstairs.

"I'll be up in time to make popcorn."

She reverted to the shy little girl who first stepped into this building with me, looking so cute as she nodded and walked out. When she glanced back from the doorway, I saw her eyebrows were furrowed in the classic Caye impatient look. I ran my fingers through my own dark brown hair and winked at her.

Courant took one of the chairs in front of my desk and I went around and sat. He pulled papers from his portfolio, laid the portfolio on the desk.

"You mentioned you charge thirty dollars per day, plus expenses. That will be fine." He leaned back in the thick chair. "Did you happen to see a movie called *Dark Heart?* Came out in '44."

"I was in Italy in '44."

"Italy?"

"Anzio. Cassino."

He nodded, looked away for a moment, like most non-vets did.

"Well," he went on, "Mr. Orson Welles produced and directed the film starring Kathy Boyer and Duane Caulkin."

"Who? I mean I heard of Welles."

"Exactly. The movie wasn't a hit."

The old man, I figured he was in his late sixties, slid two sheets of paper toward me. I had to get up to reach them. One looked like a music sheet, the other some sort of contract.

"Mr. Welles's production company did not have enough money to use an orchestra for the soundtrack, so he used recordings. I do some work for the studios and found a recording from Camp Records here in New Orleans. They're out of business now." The old man pulled a record from his portfolio. It had a blank sleeve. He put it on the desk.

"The song was used in the movie and sometimes music has a life of its own."

I looked at the lyrics on the music sheet, saw the title of the song was *How Could You Leave Me.*

Courant held up what looked like a check to show me, slipped it back into his portfolio.

"I bought the record in '42 and when the movie flopped, didn't think much about it. Camp Records went out of business right after VJ Day. Well, Crimson Records in L.A. released the song in '44 and *How Could You Leave Me* has gotten decent air time, especially back east and on the west coast, and decent sales."

I looked at the lyrics again. No author's name.

Courant stood and shoved the record to me and I reached for it. The Camp Label was sky blue with a drawing of Saint Louis Cathedral. Looked hand-drawn by a kid. Beneath the song's title was the artist Wanda Murphy. Beneath that the songwriter, A. Diluviennes. The same song was on the flip side.

"It was recorded before the war. June 1, 1940." Courant sat up. "I have checks for the artist and the songwriter. Duchess Records re-released the song with Lena Horne two months ago. It's number ten on the blues charts. Whoever this Diluviennes is has been piling up royalty money since '40."

He smiled at me and that little face suddenly looked almost young.

"I need you to find Wanda Murphy and A. Diluviennes. I can give you a five hundred dollar retainer. Don't go over it without checking with me." He slid a business card my way and I took out a notebook and ball point.

"Camp Records. You have an address?"

He gave me the address, adding, "Camp and Orange Street. River-downtown side. Office and studio in front and warehouse in back. It's closed up tight now."

"Who did you buy the record from?"

"The owner. John Livonius. He died in '46. Apparently he had no relatives, at least no one will claim him as he was in debt."

Edward Courant put a check on the edge of my desk, stood. "I look forward to hearing from you, Mr. Caye."

I walked him out, asked how he'd heard about me.

"Oh, I've heard about you for a while. You make the papers. The dick who caught public enemy number one Lou Jacobi. Albert Eindhoven doesn't like you much."

"No reason he should. I sent his son to the penitentiary." I didn't mention the little bastard should have gone to the electric chair.

Courant nodded. "Murder. There's no future in it." He grinned at me and I realized the old man had a sense of humor. I locked the building's door after he stepped out, went back to look at the check and business card. Edward Courant was an attorney-at-law. On his card he listed 'specializing in entertainment law'.

On my way upstairs, my mind flashed back to the Eindhoven Case. Couple teen-aged boys. Rich kids. Thrill killers who murdered a maid for the helluva it two years ago. Big shot lawyers got them sentenced to twenty years instead of the electric chair. The maid was 'colored' after all. Black people weren't listed as 'murdered' in the newspapers. They were 'killed'. Her name was Sadie Martin and she had a little boy named Joe-Joe.

Jeannie was on the sofa with a pillow and a light blanket, the French doors of our balcony cracked open and cool spring air flowed in the living room of my apartment, directly upstairs from my office at 909 Barracks Street, here in the lower French Quarter. The Philco was already on and some big band played *Moonlight Serenade*. The Philco radio was a console model in a spiffy walnut cabinet with large speakers that had a lot of range, low and high tones.

"It's on CBS already," Jeannie told me as I stepped into the kitchen. She had oil in the pot, a cup of popcorn kernels next to the stove. I started it up.

Jeannie and I settled on either side of the sofa with popcorn. She got a 7up and I opened an icy Falstaff as the familiar violin strains and drum-bonging theme song began and the baritone narrator with a faux British accent announced, "This is the voice of author O. Dominick McKinley welcoming you to the latest adventure of *Ella and the Pirates*.

"We last left Ella and Joe and Hannah and Owen and Debbie shipwrecked on the lost island of Santosha where, unknown to them, lay the home base of the terrible Goa Pirates …"

IT WAS LATER, after we left Ella and Owen stranded across a ravine from her friends with Goa Pirates closing in, and I carried Jeannie to bed, I came back out and put Courant's record on the Philco.

I kept it low as a guitar started up, slow strumming with a woman whispering before a sax picked up the tune then grew distant and a woman began humming, picking up the tune before her gravelly voice started in –

How could you leave our love?
How could you leave me?
How could you leave our world,
and the nights we set afire?
Our nights, Babe. Our streets, Babe
Marigny. Frenchmen. Piety and Desire

How could you leave what we had?
How could you leave our kisses?

> How could you just walk away,
> from our love, Babe?
> This was our time, Babe
> You and me and New Orleans
>
> Oh, Babe, I miss you so
> I want you mo than anything
> Come back and touch me, Babe
> Hold me, Babe
> Come to me, Babe, one more night
> Kiss me again and let my world end

I pulled up the needle. The singer's voice broke a couple times, but she recovered. Man, this woman sang with pain. I started it up again. Waited for the last stanzas that went –

> What good is my world, with you gone?
> What good is my world, if I ain't got you?
> What good is my heart without you, Babe?
> Bring back our love, Babe
> Bring back our world, Babe
> Marigny. Frenchmen. Piety and Desire

The chorus repeated twice –

> Oh, Babe, I miss you so
> I want you mo than anything
> Come back and touch me, Babe
> Hold me, Babe
> Come to me, Babe, one more night
> Kiss me again and let my world end

She controlled it better the second refrain, but her voice still quivered during the chorus. The sax haunted the background, the guitars faint, there was a drum but the woman's voice was the show. That, and the lyrics.

I'd grown to dig blues music. Muddy Waters. Little Walter. Howlin' Wolf.

So I put the song back on, stood next to the balcony door, felt the cool breeze on my face as the guitar and sax started up again. The air was sweet with rain and it came in, slowly at first, then harder and as the song ended and the Philco spun silently, the rain hammered the park and the street below, bounced on my balcony.

Bring back our love, Babe
Bring back our world, Babe
Marigny. Frenchmen. Piety and Desire

I wondered where Callie was now. She'd taken her kisses away, left our streets behind and me with a hole in my chest. If I closed my eyes I could see her pretty face, that flow of russet hair, almost feel her lips. So I did not close my eyes. Didn't want to see Callie's lips so close to mine. I looked out at the streaks of rain peppering the dark roofs of the old quarter and reminded myself. Detectives don't cry.

THE PLAN WAS for Jeannie to come with me to the library so I could check out the city and suburban directories before we went grocery shopping at the new supermarket. Needed to know if there were any listings for Wanda Murphy or A. Diluviennes and to see who lived along Camp Street from '40 to '42. The street outside was still wet, although the rain had stopped.

My black Ford sedan glistened with rain under the morning sun. Identical to an unmarked NOPD detective bureau car, my car was easily mistaken for the heat, especially by policemen. I'd even bought the police package – souped-up engine, heavy duty transmission and brakes, searchlight on the driver's side and the same, cheap hubcaps. Only Private Eyes in bad novels followed people around in flashy sports cars.

Stopping at the red light at Rampart and Canal we heard it together, a high pitched, "Meow."

I cut the engine, got out and opened the hood and a black and gray striped kitten looked up at me with big green eyes as it crouched atop the battery and went, "Meow."

We'd gone fourteen blocks with the kitten. I scooped it before it could climb away and it curled in my hand. No blood, no grease on its white belly, just a fluffy kitten. I brought it around to the passenger side as Jeannie rolled down the window and handed the kitten to her.

"Is it hurt?"

"Check it out," I said as I started back around the car. Fella in the yellow Mercury right behind my car leaned on his horn.

Yeah. Yeah.

I got going, had to make a quick U-turn to head back home.

The kitten lay curled in Jeannie's lap, staring up at her with wide eyes. She pet its belly and it started purring loud enough for me to hear.

"It was in the engine?"

"Yes and its mother's probably looking for it."

"A mother who lets her kitty climb into an engine isn't a good mother."

"Lucky it didn't get caught in the radiator fan."

My daughter's face went pale.

"Fourteen blocks," I said as we pulled up in the same parking spot in front of my building. I got out, crossed the street, looked in the park for a cat, maybe more kittens, then crossed back and stood next to my car.

"We can't just let it go. It'll get run over. It's an orphan." Jenny blinked tears from her eyes. "Like me."

I couldn't help chuckling. "You're not an orphan." I also knew – we had a kitten now.

"It's a lot of work. Litter box. Feeding it. Keeping it inside. We'll have to get it fixed at the vet and it'll have to stay inside all the time with us."

"I'll feed it."

"You'll clean the litter box?"

"Yes." Jeannie bounced in the seat. She had the kitten upright now, petting its head, holding it with the other hand.

"OK. Let's get it upstairs and when we go to the grocery, we'll get cat food and litter."

I looked around again as Jeannie climbed out with her kitten. Figured I knew the father but he was the night shift cat so he wasn't around at the moment. Not that tom cats hung around kittens.

"Is it a boy or a girl?"

I knew it was too young for us to tell so I told her the vet would know.

"If it's a boy I want to call him Harry. Like Harry Houdini, the magician. Escape artist I read about him in school."

I nodded. "If it's a girl, she can be Harri with an 'i'."

THE ESTATE OF the Tulane University President stood on the left side of Audubon Place. A massive three-story mansion with tall white Greek columns, mansion's bricks were painted the same tan color as the fieldstones of the adjoining university's main field stone buildings just down Saint Charles Avenue. A large guard shack made of identical field stone, stood in the center of the double lanes of Audubon Place. Tall, wrought gates on either side of the shack were connected to a brick wall that kept the riff-raff out of the area. The gates controlled who went in and out of the boulevard separated by a wide neutral ground – what we called medians in New Orleans. Mansions lined either side of Audubon Place, like prim manors in a make-believe world where crime was kept away by a security guard and stone wall.

The guard was a retired NOPD sergeant who had given me hell once at a crime scene when I was a rookie. He screamed at me to keep a dog away from a murder victim shot down on a street back-a-town. Later, the detectives told me that dog belonged to the victim and led them to the victim's house where they found the killer burglarizing the place.

Willie Dingle, who we called Dingleberry – God knows why – examined the letter without saying a word, checked with a list on a clipboard and let me through the gate, giving my car a sour look and I just washed the damn thing that morning. I drove slowly and noticed the cars in the long driveways were all luxury models – Lincolns, Cadillacs, Packards, a couple Mercedes, even a mint condition Duesenberg convertible with its trademark chrome grill and flared fenders.

22 Audubon Place stood in the middle of the block, a Queen Anne mansion, probably built in the Nineteenth Century. Three stories, it looked oversized for the lot and I realized the houses here were all large for their lots with long front yards but not much room between the mansions. This

mansion was predominately white with baby blue steps leading up to the first floor gallery that went around the right side of the house. The underside of the turret above the second floor balcony was also blue, another turret along the far side of the balcony had its underside painted an even paler green and the pink window shutters gave the place the look of a vanilla wedding cake.

No street parking, at least no cars were parked on the street, so I pulled into the drive behind the white Cadillac from yesterday, got out, stretched and put on my suit coat. I'd decided on my light-weight beige suit with a royal blue tie, brown and tan shoes, my snub-nosed Smith and Wesson .357 magnum in a tan holster on my right hip.

Up the twelve porch steps, I crossed to a cut-glass front door and rang the bell, which was answered quickly by a black maid in a black and white outfit. She looked at least sixty, thin, with cheeks sunken from age. Her large brown eyes were soft and she smiled and her face seemed to transform, to almost lose its deep lines.

"You must be Mr. Caye." She opened the door wider. "I'm Mary."

"Yes, ma'am." I followed her across a hardwood foyer into a thickly carpeted living room.

"Y'all have a seat and Miss Angél will be down in a moment." Pronounced as I suspected – An-jell. "Would you like iced tea or coffee?" A playful look came to her face. "We also have bourbon, scotch and three types of cold beer."

"Coffee-and-chicory?"

"Of course."

"Cream and two sugars," I said and she smiled again, left me in an airy room. This was the way a living room should be decorated, a lone sofa facing a love seat with a coffee table between. A second love seat faced the front windows.

Bookshelves filled with books. A couple lamps on small tables. Lots of open space.

Just as I was about to sit on the sofa, I spied a splash of yellow as a woman breezed in like a canary, wide yellow dress covering one of those big, bouncy slips, the kind June Allyson wore. I made a quick checklist. She was in her twenties with hair perfectly coiffured, not a strand of chestnut brown hair out of place. It was cut just above her shoulders with a slight wave. Eyes were darker brown than my brown eyes. She would be almost beautiful if those eyes weren't so small and her jaw not so large. She made up the deficiencies with expertly applied make up and dark red lipstick. The dress was linen and the necklace was a clunky gold ribbon dotted with rubies. No wedding set but the emerald ring on her right ring finger was pretty damn big. She carried another cream envelope in her hand.

"Hello there," she said as she approached. "I read about your cases in the *Eagle*. You're almost a celebrity."

Oh, Lord.

"I am Angél Brienne." The woman in yellow breezed to the love seat, waved to the sofa for me to sit. "I want you to look into a murder case from February, 1944. A former teacher of mine. He lived alone on Walnut Street. It was in the papers." She sat, put the envelope on her lap and watched me. "Were you a policeman then?"

1944. Again. Interesting. She knows I used to be a cop.

"February '44? I was in the Sideshow with the Fifth Army. Italy."

Her eyes grew even more squinty. "You were in a sideshow?"

"General Mark Clark called the Italian Campaign 'the Sideshow' as opposed to the fighting in France. Patton.

Eisenhower." I sat on the sofa, thought back to 1944, said, "February '44, I was on a beach called Anzio."

There was a hint of recognition. Infamous battles drew that kind of attention, like Iwo Jima, Normandy, Battle of the Bulge.

Mary entered with a silver tray with coffee, cream and sugar. Mine was already mixed and Angél took hers black. We each took a sip and put our cups down.

Angél smiled politely, said, "I gather my retainer was sufficient."

"I charge thirty a day, plus mileage and expenses. A grand goes a long way."

"Good. I don't want a rush job." She leaned forward, slid the new envelope across the coffee table to me, nodded to it. I picked it up, found two sheets of the same stationery with plenty of typing.

She picked up her coffee. "His name was Sullivan Slushy. The New Orleans Police won't even talk to me about the case."

I began reading the first page of her letter. Sullivan was fifty-two at the time he was found shot to death in his house.

"They closed the case," she added. "Pinned it on a man who died in prison two years ago. Died of cancer. But he did not kill Sullivan."

"You sure about that?"

"I have a lead. His wife did it."

"Thought you said this Sullivan lived alone?"

"They were estranged. She was an actress in a traveling summer stock production troupe." Angél nodded to the papers in my hand. "I have her information in there."

There was a list of names and addresses on Walnut Street.

"I know she did it because I have been inquiring of the neighbors and they say it is common knowledge in the neighborhood." She pointed at the note in my hand. "I do not know how to take statements, which is what my lawyer said is needed. He said a private investigator was needed and could recommend one."

"Who is your lawyer?"

"Abraham Rubenstein."

Of *Rubenstein, Rubenstein, Rubenstein and Rubenstein.* Never met any but who hasn't heard of those guys? I think Abraham was the first one.

"They recommended *me*?"

She smiled, leaned back and crossed her legs, smoothing her dress now.

"You don't remember me, do you?"

Oh, no.

"Should I?" I was sure I had never put a move on this woman so why was I squirming? Glad I deposited the retainer check on the way over.

"May 1940. You were a policeman back then. Two girls escaped from The Academy in revealing night clothes. You found us at Lee Circle."

"Nightgown girls?"

"I was fourteen."

I remembered a strawberry blond in a see-through negligee who knew it was sheer and wasn't shy about it. Angél must have been the other girl. Another negligee but not as sheer.

"I was with Fanny Steele. She has always been a little on the trampy side. We're still best friends."

Trampy? No wonder. Her parents named her Fanny. Wonder how someone could look at a beautiful newborn and says, "Yep. That's Fanny."

Angél leaned close, lowered her voice, "Fanny got pregnant our senior year and went away to have the baby." Angél straightened up. "She's done all right, married a doctor. Her father is still chief of security for Shell Oil on Gravier Street."

I was reading the names of the women Angél had spoken to who knew Slushy was murdered by his wife. All lived on Walnut Street. I wouldn't start there, of course. I knew exactly where to start with this case. The Detective Bureau.

It took me an hour to extricate myself from Angél who bantered about The Academy mostly. Academie de Jeanne d'Arc, everyone called The Academy, was the city's most exclusive all-girls school, grades from Kindergarten through high school, two stately buildings behind a six foot brick wall along Saint Charles Avenue's Garden District. Most of the students boarded there. The Arcasian nuns in huge white head-dresses, looked like a seagull perched on their head, were allegedly great teachers and frankly, some tough gals.

No one climbed that fence except for the occasionally rebellious girl, like Angél and Fanny. I'd heard of two cases of boys trying to sneak in on the girls and two occasions of burglars – all caught by the Arcasians who eventually called NOPD to come and untie the burglars who pleaded to be taken to parish prison or the state penitentiary, anywhere, just get them the hell away from the nuns.

"You won't believe what they did to me," one particular burglar told me when we fetched him.

I laughed. "You're looking for sympathy from the *police?*"

I LEFT A message at the Detective Bureau, then headed to the public library and wound up copying pages from the 1940 through 1947 City Directory for the blocks of Camp and Orange Streets. Found Camp Records, then found a home phone listing for John Livonius on Erato Street, which went away in 1947. Year after he died. Found no Wanda Murphy, but three W. Murphys. No Diluviennes in any of the directories.

I used a pay phone outside the library and spoke with a Mrs. William Murphy whose husband was a dentist and Mrs. Weldon Murphy, a war widow. Neither woman was a singer. The third W. Murphy number didn't answer. I took a hunch and called Livonius's old number, woke up a man who said it was a wrong number and hung up on me.

Next stop, NOPSI on Baronne Street. New Orleans Public Service, Inc., the electric company that also billed the gas company. No luck with Wanda Murphy or any Diluviennes. My contact at the phone company confirmed no unlisted numbers for either name.

PICKED UP A couple burgers with thick French fries from the Clover Grill and beat the rain home as it moved in from the lake. Red-faced Jeannie was on the sofa with her kitten which looked like a limp noodle and I wondered who wore out who.

"Who was watching you?"

"Miss Kaye."

I scooped my phone, called Kaye Rudabaugh, our new building manager, told her I was home.

"She give you any trouble?"

Jeannie's eyebrows raised.

"No," Kaye answered. "Cute kitten."

They took turns watching Jeannie. The eighty-something year old Englishman across the hall, John Stanford, had taken on the role of uncle, while twenty-year old Kaye Rudabaugh had become a big sister. Jeannie helped with Kaye's little

Hold Me, Babe

Donna, now a precocious three-year old. It was a cozy apartment building with my office right below.

Why do I always worry it'll all come crashing down?

Strange. No. Not strange at all. I've seen too much of the ugly side to know good things don't last.

Jeannie and I watched TV with the kitten who recovered nicely from its exhaustion, ate, took a drink of water, went to the litter box before coming back to pounce on us on the sofa. We started with a pretty bad show of futuristic fighters for truth and justice – *Captain Video and his Video Rangers*, who wore what looked like surplus army uniforms with lightning bolts sewn on. Jeannie thought the teen-aged Video Ranger who seemed to have no name, was cute.

This was followed by the incredibly bad puppet show called *Kukla, Fran and Ollie.*

Thankfully there was a re-run of last Saturday night's *Your Show of Shows* with the hilarious Sid Caesar, Carl Reiner and Howard Morris and the funniest-homeliest woman on the planet – Imogene Coca. Jeannie got bored and took her kitten to bed.

A half hour later my doorbell rang and I hit the buzzer, went out on the landing to see Lieutenant Frenchy Capdeville trailing cigarette smoke up the stairs. He stepped into the living room, went straight to the ash tray I'd put on the coffee table and put out his cig as I moved to the kitchen for a couple cold *smiles* – beer, as he calls it.

"Gimme a cold smile," was Frenchy's usual greeting, followed by "Pretty Baby." Only person to ever call me that. Envision Zorro – the Tyrone Power version – but not as pretty-boy and with a wide Cajun nose, and that was Frenchy.

He dropped a manila folder on the coffee table as I popped the cap off two icy bottles of Falstaff.

"I didn't work the case," he said. "Jailhouse confession is in there. Not much to it. Man said he did it only ..."

"Only what?"

"Ever hear of a Harlow .32 caliber revolver?"

"Nope."

"Me either. Made in Singapore. Pre-war, obviously." He took a hit of beer, made a face. I would have as well if I hadn't known the beer was icy cold. I'd put a six pack in the freezer when I got home. Frenchy went on, "The lands and grooves inside the barrel of a Harlow are even more unique than most revolvers. According to our firearms experts, Sullivan Slushy was shot with a Harlow. Close range."

"OK."

Frenchy nodded at the manila folder. "Jailhouse confessor couldn't remember what kind of gun he used. Said he got it from a fella on the street."

"OK."

"Harlow is the only revolver I heard of with an *automatic* safety. Close the cylinder after loading and you have to twist off the safety *and* it's not a double action revolver."

"Which meant the shooter had to twist off the safety and cock the hammer to fire it."

"He was asked about the gun. Said what we all say. There's no safety on a revolver."

I stated the obvious. "He didn't know the Harley."

"Harlow. Zactly."

"So you think the jailhouse confession ..."

"Is bullshit. He also confessed to two rapes and three armed robberies. I went on vacation and the other squad cleared six cases with one confession."

"Haverton?"

"Of course."

We both took a swig. No need to bash the incompetent Detective Alvin Haverton. Man was killed by a drunk driver last year. He was the drunk driver. Hit an oak tree on Carrollton Avenue at sixty miles an hour.

"What about the victim's wife?" I asked Frenchy.

He grinned at me, his feet up on my coffee table now.

"That's your play now, ain't it? I'm working two homicides at the moment."

"SHE INHERITED THE place," said the woman holding a martini glass in her left hand, other hand on her door so she could shut it quickly, no doubt. The woman's blurry eyes looked at me through cat-eyed glasses. She looked to be around forty, wore a pink dress and low black heels. This was Nancy Hanks who lived two doors down Webster Street from murder victim Sullivan Slushy's house. Running along the uptown side of Audubon Park the houses on the even side of the street, like the victim's, had the park as a vast backyard.

"The wife inherited the place?"

"Yeah. The wife. She spent what, a year in jail for murdering her husband?" A crooked smile crept across her face and Nancy Hanks took a sip of martini. "If I did such a thing, they'd lock me up and throw away the key. Not that it isn't tempting. You married?"

"Yes, ma'am," I lied.

I'd left my suit coat in the car, thankfully, and felt perspiration working its way down my back. Nancy Hanks was the first name on Angél's list so I asked if she remembered speaking to Angél about the case.

"Huh?"

I described Angél and the woman nodded, took another sip of martini. "Yes. She was at the Schultz party. We told her all about it."

"Do you know for sure the man's wife went to jail for the murder?"

Nancy Hanks furrowed her brow, took a sip of martini and said, "Now that you mention it – no."

"Where did you hear it?"

She shrugged, took another sip of martini.

I found Barbara Schultz next door. She also wore pink, slacks and matching blouse, but wasn't drinking. She blew cigarette smoke from the corner of her mouth in a fine straight stream, sucked on her cigarette between breaths and told me she'd heard it all from Ida Lupin across the street. Ida was in as well and spoke to me in her doorway, just like the others. She told me she'd heard the story from the widow Slushy herself.

"What did she say?"

"She inherited the house."

"I mean about the murder."

"Oh, she didn't mention the murder."

What?

"Where did you see her?"

"Ran into her coming out of D. H. Holmes last Christmas. We talked a good fifteen minutes."

I took a chance, went to the victim's house, rang the bell and a thin woman wearing a green blouse and black slacks answered the door. She looked at the business card I held out for her, took it and I stepped back. The house was one story with a pitched roof, looked a little like a Swiss Chalet. Mostly blond brick with some wooden sections and a green tile roof.

"Mrs. Slushy?"

"No. Mrs. Hansen. I'm Eileen Hansen." She looked at my card, "Mr. Caye." She looked at my side. "Sam Spade carries a gun. Don't you?"

"It's in my car. Didn't think I'd need one talking to ladies."

"Well, I'm not much of a lady but I got a better sounding name than Slusher. You have the wrong house."

I looked at my notes. This was the address on the police report and Angél's note.

I took another step back. Giving distance to a woman who stood a half foot smaller than me. It seemed to relax her.

"How long have you lived here, ma'am?"

"Nine months. My husband is a river pilot. His name isn't Slusher either."

I looked around, backed up again and thanked her. "Sorry, wrong address." I stopped, asked, "Would you happen to have a forwarding address for the previous owner?"

"No."

I left a message with Mary for Angél, piddled around my office, got an answer at the third W. Murphy number from the City Directory. The one who didn't answer yesterday. A man said he was Wally Murphy and didn't know any Wanda. He hung up on me.

I watched Jeannie step out of the school bus at the corner and come running to the front door. She was half way up the stairs by the time I reached the foyer.

"What's the hurry?"

"Gotta check on the kitty."

Later, just as I was pulling my feet off my desk to head upstairs for supper, Angél called. I gave her the rundown. Her leads from her lush friends didn't amount to much.

"What will you do now?"

"Find the widow. She still shops at Holmes. So she's still in town."

I called upstairs and Jeannie answered, "Caye residence."

"I'm going around the corner for po-boys. You want your usual?" French-fry po-boy dripping with roast beef gravy.

"Positively. With extra gravy."

"Is Mr. Stanford with you?"

"Yes."

"Tell him I'm getting him his usual." The Englishman couldn't resist a roast beef po-boy.

"OK. And can you get some boiled shrimp for the kitty?"

"No. That's why God invented cat food."

"God didn't invent cat food."

"How do you know?"

"Because it's not in the Gospel."

Oh, Lord. I asked for that one.

The cat on the night shift, Mister black and white, stood atop the fence again when I came out to walk to Bessie Lee's Café and Bar. He pretended he wasn't watching me but when I looked back over my shoulder, I saw him staring. I was, after all, another tom cat on his turf.

AFTER CHECKING THE most obvious place, the latest phone book for Mrs. Slushy, Wanda Murphy and any Diluviennes – don't laugh, finding witnesses for lawyers too lazy to pick up a phone book was like finding money on the street, which I'd done more than once. Better because a lawyer just gave the money to me. I went to city hall and got a copy of the marriage license of Sullivan E. Slushy and Myrtle A. Littonel, dated April 1, 1926. While I was at vital records, I got a copy of Angél's birth certificate. I needed to know more about the Briennes and her father's name was Ernest, her mother was Hilda Frenier.

Hold Me, Babe

My sources with NOPD and NOPSI showed no record of any Myrtle Littonel or Myrtle Slushy. She's never had electricity or gas in her name, which meant she lived with her parents until she married back in '26 and moved away after the death of her late husband. She might have been from out of town as there was no one with the last name Littonel in any of the listings for power, telephone, arrests. Next step, re-check the phone book for Littonels. I did. None listed.

Orleans Parish conveyance records gave me the name of the real estate agent who handled the sale of the Slushy house on Walnut Street nine months ago. Roberts Realty, located on Dublin Street a block off Leake Avenue and the river levee, occupied a one story wooden building that used to be someone's house before businesses crept into the neighborhood.

Richard Roberts wasn't in, but his secretary was married to a Jefferson Parish sheriff's deputy and slipped me the forwarding address used by Myrtle Slushy at the act of sale. I tried not to react to seeing the address, thanking the nice secretary and passing her a card, telling her that if I could return the favor for her or her cop husband, call me.

Standing next to my Ford, I put on my dark sunglasses and looked up toward the sun, felt its heat on my face for a moment before looking back at my notes. The forwarding address used by Myrtle Slushy was 22 Audubon Place.

Sometimes, I feel like I'm a living cliché, having to scrape gum from my Florsheims. This is why we're called Gumshoes – picking up gum as we walk from place to place. Shamus, Snoop, Sleuth, Private Eye. Lot of detail work. Not as glamorous as in the movies.

I climbed into my car and meandered back home in the lower French Quarter, wondering what I knew of the Brienne family except they owned a mansion and a white Cadillac and Angél paid me good money to discover her 'lead' was bogus and the person she thought was the killer used her house as a forwarding address.

Which left me with the rest of the Brienne family. Who the hell was I dealing with? No doubt these were society people and the total tonnage of what I knew about society people couldn't fill a – but I knew someone who would know.

I DROPPED BY the Central Grocery to pick up a muffuletta for supper, asked my buddy Dino Nuzzolillo if he'd ever heard of a singer named Wanda Murphy or anyone named Diluviennes. He knew the New Orleans music scene a lot better than me.

"Never heard of Wanda Murphy or that other name."

"She was a Blues singer."

He shook his head. "Maybe in the Negro joints." He gave me his big smile. "You should come with me sometime. Cool music, man."

Jeannie Marie Caye was partial to muffulettas and she bounced off the sofa when I told her what was in the brown paper sack. The kitten stood up on the sofa, stretched, curled its back and went "Meow" when Jeannie headed into the kitchen to help me.

"Did you get French fries too?"

She was also partial to the Central Grocery's thick fries. She was still in her school uniform so I asked if she got her homework done.

"Kaye helped me."

As I laid out a quarter of muffuletta for each of us on my Formica kitchen table – I wondered how many Private Eyes worried about homework. I had to cut Jeannie's quarter into smaller slices and we dipped fries into ketchup and ate our sandwich in silence, her grinning at me between bites, having to wipe olive oil dripping from her mouth.

For those never blessed to eat in New Orleans – a muffuletta sandwich was invented here at the Central Grocery. Large and thick, round Italian bread was sliced horizontally through the center, laid open and slathered in olive oil before layers of ham, salami and several different cheeses is topped with homemade olive salad then cut into quarters.

We settled on the sofa in time for *Ella and the Pirates*. Apparently Ella and Owen had managed to shove the half-rotted tree they used to cross a great ravine into the precipice, leaving frustrated, murderous Goa Pirates on the other side of the ravine as Ella and Owen raced away.

I finally got around to my newspaper and the headline on *The Eagle* read: Rosenbergs Guilty! There really wasn't much doubt about it. Stealing the US atomic bomb secrets and giving them to the Soviet Union was the worse news since Pearl Harbor. The article speculated old Julius and Ethel would be executed. The accompanying photo did nothing to draw sympathy, with Ethel's lips pursed in almost a smile on her chubby face and her bespectacled husband looking too much like Heinrich Himmler.

I moved to the sports page to check on my Yankees, found an article about the youngster set to replace the irreplaceable Joe DiMaggio. Kid named Mickey Mantle. For the first time in their history, The New York Yankees went west for spring training – Arizona and California. The world champs, who had swept the Phillies in last year's World Series, were favored to repeat. But that was the usual story. Mantle wasn't.

"The kid ain't logical," complained Manager Casey Stengel. "He's too good. It's very confusing."

The article went on to remind us of the symmetry in the Yankees line of succession. It was Lou Gehrig who followed Babe Ruth into superstardom. DiMaggio debuted at the end of Gehrig's career. Not that Joltin' Joe was finished in '51, after all he blasted 32 homers last year, along with 122 RBIs, but Mantle was a *phenom*. Besides, Mickey Mantle was a shortstop. Apparently, an incredibly good switch-hitter.

The kitten decided to dive through the newspaper as I held it up, tumbling into my lap and scrambling, little claws shredding the page as it climbed up to my neck and went, "Yowl. Yowl."

ANNIE FORDOW HAD taken over the Society section of *The Eagle* while I was dodging bombs in Italy. We'd dated a couple times before the war but she found a guy she was more interested in, a fellow Holy Cross Tiger – Big Billy Fordow, who was a guard on our football team while I was a halfback. I'd spotted her name on the column and this was my first call to what I hoped would become a good source.

"Lunch?" she said when I called shortly after nine. "What for?"

"Food." I laughed. "Annie, I need some help with a society matter and you do eat lunch don't you?"

"Sometimes."

"Let me buy you lunch."

"OK. I guess."

"What's the problem?"

"When I told Billy we had dated he wasn't happy about it. Said you were a lothario."

"A what?"

"A Don Juan. Casanova."

"Did we even kiss?" As soon as I said it, I regretted it.

"Goodnight. We kissed goodnight. Twice. You don't remember kissing me?"

"I meant French kiss. You know. Heavy stuff."

"Oh." She didn't sound convinced but agreed to meet me around the corner from *The Eagle*. Little place called Café Beaucaire where we had a couple roast beef po-boys. Annie took mayonnaise on her quarter loaf. I ordered a half loaf of the French bread sandwich, no mayo, just extra gravy. We both tucked napkins under our chins, not out of the ordinary in New Orleans, especially when eating gravy drippy po-boys. I waited until we were into it before asking about the Brienne family.

"You have no clue who they are do you?"

"That's right." I grinned at Annie who shook her head.

"Old money. Been here long before the Louisiana Purchase. Families like Louvier, Raveneaux, Monlezun and Brienne were the city's wealthiest. Still are. They don't gamble with stocks and bonds. They own property. Do you know who owns the most property in the French Quarter?"

I knew that answer, but just shrugged.

"The archdiocese. You think the Catholic church doesn't know how to make and keep money? They don't even pay any taxes."

"I heard of Raveneaux Jewelers and don't the Louviers own a bank?"

"Several."

"And the Briennes?"

"They own Audubon Place. Most of the houses are actually long-term family leases because people like the Briennes don't sell land. Ever. They have property all over town. Office buildings and a couple wharves."

"What do you know about Ernest Brienne?"

"He doesn't socialize much since his wife died during the war. Cancer. His father dabbled in bootlegging until he got a three a.m. visit at his Audubon Place mansion by Peter Piazza, himself. He wasn't the boss back then, probably a capo."

"That's when they put up the guard shack and fence?"

"The guard was there. You don't think that could keep the Mafia out. Old man Brienne bragged about it for years, waking up with Mafia thugs standing in his bedroom. Apparently it was only a veiled threat and Brienne was smart enough to quit dabbling and buy the liquor for his restaurants from Piazza's crew. Oh, yeah. The Briennes own some restaurants too. The Soames Plantation on the lakefront and The Azalea Court in the Quarter.

Swanky places.

I nodded. Gave me some perspective before I went back to ask Angél why the woman she thought was a murderer used the Brienne address as a forwarding address. If I could find Myrtle Littonel Slushy first, that would be even better. But how?

"Have you ever heard of a singer named Wanda Murphy?"

"No."

"Anybody named Diluviennes?"

"Spell that."

I did.

She shook her head, said, "Diluviennes means 'torrential' in French."

ONLY PLACE TO go was back to Walnut Street after lunch, after Annie told me a couple recent society stories that she couldn't put into print. Nothing too outrageous, just two teen-agers joyriding with the family's Bentley committing a couple hit-and-runs and a wandering daughter caught stripping at a Bourbon Street nightclub.

I checked. Her name wasn't Fanny.

Just before four, I gave up on Walnut Street. Not a person on either side of the street was friends with Myrtle or Sullivan for that matter. Friendly, but not friends enough to have kept up with the widow after the death.

A different guard at the Audubon Place gate, another old timer, wasn't impressed with the ten I tried to give him to call the Brienne house to allow me in. I don't trust people who don't take tips. He grumbled but called when I wouldn't go away and mispronounced my name. He finally let me through.

The white Cadillac sat in the driveway, along with a black Rolls Royce and a wine-colored '50 Lincoln Continental. Mary let me in. Whatever was cooking in the kitchen in back smelled wonderful.

I recognized the strawberry blond sitting on the sofa across from Angél. Fanny Steele picked up her martini glass and smiled at me as she took a sip and Angél introduced us.

"I remember you, Mr. Caye. Although you may not recognize me."

"Lee Circle. How could I forget?"

"I didn't realize you actually looked at my face that night." Fanny giggled. "We were naughty girls that evening."

I had looked at her face but that's not what I remembered.

Fanny ended up tall, around five-nine, and lovely in a dark green dress that made her hair look radiant. Her wedding set had a huge diamond, and her gold necklace was dotted with emeralds, so was its matching bracelet. She'd done well. Angél said she'd married a doctor.

"Didn't realize you had company," I said as Mary brought me a cup of coffee-and-chicory with cream and two sugars. I thanked her.

"You sure you don't want a martini?" Angél asked. She was dressed up in pink chiffon.

"Mary's got it right." I took a sip of coffee, said, "If y'all are going out, I'll make this short."

"Oh, no. We're waiting supper. We've been shopping all day."

I asked if I could have a word in private with Angél.

"If it's about the case, go ahead. I have no secrets from Fanny."

"Case?" Fanny asked.

"Mr. Caye is a Private Eye now and he's looking into the Sullivan Slushy Case."

Angél may not keep secrets from Fanny but the look on Fanny's face showed she wasn't privy to this yet. She sat up stiffer, held on to the martini glass with both hands. I positioned myself, still standing, away from them so I could see both reactions when I said, "I spoke to all the women on your list and some others. No one has any information about the case so I've been looking for the widow." I took a sip of coffee. "She sold the house but she's still in town."

"Do you know where she is?" asked Angél.

"Is your father in?"

"He's upstairs."

"You think I could speak with him?"

A car engine started and I moved to the curtains and dammit, I should have parked behind the Rolls. It backed out and pulled away.

Angél was next to me now with the scent of My Sin.

"I wonder where Papa's going?"

I was tempted to run out and try to follow the old man, but the guard would be in no hurry to open the gate for me. Glad I didn't say anything about the forwarding address. Yet.

MY OFFICE PHONE rang as I came downstairs the next morning, and kept ringing.

"Hello."

"Hello, Lucien." A soft female voice I'd heard before but couldn't place.

"It's Helen Bern, Lucien. Can you drop by this morning?"

Flashes of ash blond hair and a face expertly made up, scarlet lips against snowy skin and large brown eyes. A tall woman in a prim suit. She was a couple years older than me, but not many.

"This morning? I guess so."

"Come through the side gate. Bye, now."

A former client. Couple years ago, I helped Helen Bern recover a bracelet stolen by one of her maids. Wasn't hard to do, actually. Felt sorry for the maid in the end, so much I gave her a head start before I tipped the police. She took it and blew town and as the day shift tomcat watched me pull away in my Ford, I sure hoped the idiot maid hadn't returned.

Helen lived in the Garden District on Prytania Street in a three story mansion, an ante-bellum Greek revival painted bright white, half-hidden by towering magnolia trees and a garden. As I recalled, her husband had run off with a gypsy long before she called for my help with the bracelet. I didn't know we had gypsies in Louisiana.

I took the side gate into the garden and moved through the delightful scent of pink blooming azaleas, camellia bushes some with white flowers, some red and wide, tall crepe myrtles, with pale pink blossoms. The scents stronger from red and white rose bushes.

The portico alongside the house allowed cars to pull from Prytania, drop off visitors and exit along the side street. Helen answered the doorbell, a small brandy snifter in her hand. She wore an evening gown, white, long, satin, slim. She also wore the once purloined bracelet I'd returned to her.

"Thank you for coming, Lucien."

She bumped cheeks with me, kissing the air next to my ear and I smelled Chanel No. 5. She turned and I followed her hips through a small foyer, into a hall and turned into her large living room with its wall of French doors facing Prytania.

Too much furniture – three sofas, two love seats, a grand piano, two cuckoo clocks, a roll-top desk, miscellaneous arm chairs, antique coffee table and a wet bar – but the room was big enough, I suppose. The rugs looked Persian and the room smelled of more flowers.

She slipped to the wet bar, asked if I'd like something to drink.

At nine a.m.?

"No, thanks."

"I'll never have another white maid." She waved her wrist with bracelet, poured another shot of brown liquid into her snifter from a decanter, came over and waved me to a blue sofa. She walked past, showing me her fine lines, giving me another whiff of Chanel No. 5 as she went to a large phonograph, bigger than my Philco and put on an album. Classical music. An orchestra sounding like it was in a hurry.

"Prokofiev."

Sure.

Didn't I see a Bugs Bunny cartoon with this music, Elmer Fudd and Viking women with swords?

Helen came and sat at the other end of the sofa, reached down and took off her heels. She closed her eyes and let the music flow over us.

I waited for whatever was on her mind.

"I've been thinking about you, Lucien. Have you been thinking about me?"

"Yes," I lied. *What else could I say? No, lady. Haven't given you a thought.*

I waited for it.

When the song ended and another began, her eyes opened and she took a sip of her liquor and put the glass on the coffee table, kept those big browns on me as she pulled her legs up and draped them across my lap.

OK. What this? As if I didn't know.

"I want you to do something for me, Lucien."

I tried not to squirm when she drew her left foot over my crotch.

"I want you to do me. Upstairs. Now." Her left eye narrowed. "Make me call you God."

How the hell did I not laugh? 'Do me? Make me call you God'.

She rubbed her foot against my erection.

Who was I argue with a lady?

I traced my fingers up her leg, all the way to her smooth thigh, shoving up the dress and she lifted her other knee, let it fall to show she wasn't wearing anything under the dress. A natural blond, her bush looked fluffy and when she opened her legs to slowly climb off, her pink slit looked almost wet.

She took my hand and led me through the room to the spiral staircase and up to her bedroom to a huge, four-posted bed, pulled me to it. She went up on her toes in front of me and brushed her lips across mine, kissed me then we French kissed, her hands wrapping around my neck, my hands cupping her ass.

We came up for air and stood a foot apart, undressing one another, eyes occasionally meeting. A sly smile came to her lips with her dress pooled at her feet. She had no trouble getting me naked, except for socks and shoes.

"Should we close the door?" I asked.

"The help isn't around. It's just you and little ole me." She pointed to the dresser. "Trojans in the top right drawer." I pulled out three rubbers, just in case, dressed my dick with one.

Helen moved around to the far side of the bed, climbed on, kneeled there moving her hands behind her head to give me a good look at her body, firm round breasts, not oversized but creamy white with pale pink areoles and small nipples pointed in anticipation. She rolled on her side and lay on her back and I went to the end of the bed climbed up as she opened her legs for me.

I kissed and licked my way back and forth up each smooth leg up to her thighs. I nibbled each and moved to her bush, kissed her silky hair, let my tongue flick against her clit and then kissed her. I made love to her 'with my face' as the French say it.

She cried and gasped and bounced and I kept it up until she came and fell back and said, "Now. Now. Now."

I know. Do me.

So I did her. Then did her again. And she did call me God each time.

Lying next to one another, our bodies recovering, air-conditioned air cooling us, Helen kissed my lips again and climbed off.

"Let's shower. I have to go to Temple later."

"Temple?"

"You didn't know I'm Jewish?"

"Not really. How am I supposed to know that?"

She shrugged. "Some people go out of their way to find out."

"Who? Germans?" I moved over. "It's not my business, people's religion." I kissed her. "Whatever belief brought you to drag me into your bed, I'm all for."

"The religion of passion."

"Yeah. That sounds good."

It was a walk-in shower and we washed each other off. Back in the bedroom, she stepped up and kissed me again, softly. With her makeup washed off, she looked washed out, but pretty as hell with her hair wet.

"It's going to take me a while to get made-up after you wrecked me, Lucien." She patted my chest.

As I got dressed she added, "It was nice. Very nice."

She's telling me?

I kissed the nape of her neck and left her there.

Moving through the garden I knew I had to think about this. I wanted to let it just flow, like a river, right past me. She needed doing and I was the instrument. But why? Why today?

Shut up, Lucien. Just go with it. I'd been neglecting my libido for a while and I shouldn't. After all, I was a lothario, wasn't I?

MY VISITOR CAME at two-thirty in the morning and it wasn't the Mafia. I went out on the balcony and leaned over to see a tall man in dark clothes leaning on my doorbell. All I could see was the top of his head and there was a bald spot there. I went in to check Jeannie and she was a heavy sleeper, thankfully. The kitty stood up next to her, wide eyes watching me, ears straight up.

In undershirt and denim pants, I slipped into tennis shoes, brought my Colt .45 automatic and an extra clip for good measure and went downstairs and out the door along the Dauphine Street side of the building, walked across Barracks Street to the wall along the park. The man stepped away from the doorbell, looked up at my balcony.

The gaslight under the balcony showed me a man in his fifties, thin, with gray hair and wearing a gray shirt and black pants. He took a nickel-plated revolver from his pocket, scratched his nose with the muzzle.

I crept across the street as he moved back to the doorbell. I tip-toed up behind him, raised my .45 and slammed it hard against the hand holding his revolver and it fell to the lone step up to the building's front door. He wheeled and I caught his jaw with a left hook and he went straight down. I picked up the revolver with my left hand. It was a big gun, six-inch barrel, pointed the .45 at the man's nose and said, "What the fuck you want, ass-hole?"

He started to get up. "You live here?"

I pushed him back down with my foot.

"Who you looking for?"

"Goddamn snooping Private Eye." His cheeks were sunken and his eyes bulged.

"You're talking to him. Who are you?" I didn't picture Angél's father looking like this.

"Stay away from my daughter!" He started to get up again.

"Stay down. Who is your daughter?"

"You know who."

Where the hell was a prowl car when you need a cop?

"Mister. I see a lot of people every day. Including people's daughters."

He tried to get up again and I shoved my pistol against his nose.

"This is a Colt 1911 model, .45 caliber automatic. I'll blow your head off, you keep moving."

He started breathing harder and I thought – *don't have a cardiac on me.* I should have called the police from my apartment. I didn't want to kill an angry old man, especially if he was one of the most prominent men in town.

"Stay away from Fanny! This is the only warning you'll get. I'll hire someone next time. You won't see it coming."

Fanny? Fanny.

I stepped back. "You bring a gun to my house again and Fanny'll have to bury you."

He snarled at me

"I'll shoot first next time." I backed down the banquette. "And I don't miss what I shoot at, you dipshit."

I thought of following him, make sure he left but I didn't. He got up slowly and walked up the street, turned the corner up at Burgundy and I spotted the cat on the night shift cross Barracks Street, heading for the playground.

I went through the front door, making sure it locked behind me.

Jeannie was still asleep, her kitten curled next to her so I went back into the living room, took a cold Falstaff and the dipshit's revolver to my sofa. The transoms above the French doors were still open, letting in a cool breeze scented with the musty smell of the lower Quarter. Dust. A hint of mildew. The scent of old wood slowly losing its strength.

The revolver was a nickel-plated Harlow .32 caliber. Boxy. Oversized top rail. Safety on its left side. If this was *the* gun, it was the first time a murder weapon was hand-delivered to me. I unloaded it, left the cylinder open and put it and the bullets in a brown paper bag to give to Frenchy.

Back on my sofa, I sipped the cool beer.

What did I know of Fanny's father? Last name was Steele and he was some sort of security manager for Gulf Oil. No. Shell Oil. And he was an angry man, angry enough to bring a pistol to see a Private Eye.

I DROPPED THE Harlow pistol off at the Detective Bureau for Frenchy to get the firearms examiner to compare to the Slushy murder weapon. Hell, I might have solved a murder for him. I should have gotten a ticket, parking in a police zone but the cop on the beat probably mistook my Ford for a prowl car and – no ticket.

So I headed to Camp Street. I did have another case to work. Edward Courant was right. The building at the river-downtown corner of Camp and Orange Street was boarded up tight.

In New Orleans, we never give directions as North, South, East or West. The city lies on a wide crescent along the Mississippi River, which makes the west bank of the river at the French Quarter actually East of the city at uptown. The west bank is south of most of the city. Since the lake is always above the city and the river always below, running down to the Gulf of Mexico, upriver is uptown and downriver is downtown. Hence, the building I was looking at was on the river side of Camp Street and the downtown side of Orange Street. It's important when you're a cop and have to fix a location in a report. Trust me on this.

A light breeze fluttered the peeling yellow paint of the two story wooden building. The small sign above the front door, which faced Camp Street, was missing a letter and read CAMP ECORDS. Up close I saw the 'R' had been scratched away and a five pointed star carved in its place. A second floor window was broken and the first floor windows too grimy to see inside.

I went up the front steps of the house next door, a shotgun double, and knocked on the first door. No answer. The other door was answered by an ancient woman wearing a long robe and a nightcap from a Dickens novel. She said she was happy the noisy bastards next door went out of business.

"All form of creatures came in and out of there."

"Creatures?"

"Beatniks, jigaboos, Mexicans." She leaned close and I smelled pickles. "One of them had a watermelon-head."

Could she provide any names, contact information, I asked. She looked at me as if I had a watermelon-head.

The neighborhood was more run-down than my digs in the Lower Quarter. Pot-holed streets, kids running around in shorts and dirty undershirts when they should be in school. Mine was the newest car in the area. The finer homes a few blocks away along Coliseum Square were faded shadows of Gilded Age glory. It was as if the neighborhood was holding its breath to see which way it would go. Up or down, now that we were in the first year of the second half of the 20th Century.

Time for more gumshoe work, knocking on every door in the area. Starting on Camp Street. I was thinking I needed shoes with rubber soles by the time I knocked on the door of the third house along the uptown side of Orange Street where I found Mrs. Ludmilla Singleton who was once Mrs. Ludmilla Livonius. Sometimes persistence paid off. I think Philip Marlowe said that. Might have been Daffy Duck.

"Haven't seen a man around here in a suit in years," Ludmilla said from behind her locked screen door. She was a short person, nearly as wide as she was tall, with a pretty face and large brown eyes. She wore a purple print dress with a skinny black belt and flat shoes, held a broom in her hand. The gold bandana atop her head hid most of her light brown hair.

"I have a lawyer," she said. "I'm not responsible for my ex-husband's debts."

"I'm trying to find one of your ex-husband's singers. And a songwriter. Wanda Murphy and A. Diluviennes."

"Never heard of them. If they sang for him they were either wannabe entertainers or drug addicts at the end of their dream to be an entertainer."

"Are there any company records?"

"Plenty. Warehouse behind the place has plenty records. Melting in the heat."

"I mean written records. Financial records."

"You find any, let me know. My lawyer's given up."

I took in a deep breath. My right foot was aching for some reason.

"Do you know anyone else connected with Camp Records that I can speak with?"

She shook her head, moved closer to the screen, those eyes looking hard at me.

"Would you like a cup of coffee. Something stronger?"

"No, thanks." I pulled out a business card and dropped it into the black mailbox next to her door. "If you find anyone that could help me, I'd appreciate a call."

"I might do that." She licked her upper lip, slowly.

ON MY WAY home, I dropped by Joey's Records on Rampart Street. Had to squeeze past three teen-aged girls and a boy leafing through records in the narrow store while Fats Domino sang *The Fat Man* in the background. The place smelled of bubble gum, better than the beer stink outside. The record store lay sandwiched between bars.

Joey stood next to his cash register, a smallish, thin man with curly salt-and-pepper hair and wore a black T-shirt, black slacks and dark sunglasses.

"Yeah, man," he said when I stepped up. "Fats is the coolest, man. He's from N'Awlins, you know, Daddy."

I knew. Everyone knew.

"You have Lena Horn's *How Could You Leave Me?*"

"Sure do, Daddy-O." He hurried around the counter to the far aisle and half-way down, brought back a record, handed it to me. A. Diluviennes was listed as songwriter on the Duchess label as well. The flip side was a song *Curvaceous Brunette*, songwriter J. Dickens.

"You wanna hear it?"

I handed it back and he put it on a turntable and this was a well-polished version of the song. Lena's voice was deeper but lacked the sadness in Wanda's version. The orchestra accompanying Lena drew out the range of her voice and it was a nice record.

When Joey passed it back, I pointed to the label and asked about A. Diluviennes.

"Never heard of the name. Sounds Lithuanian."

It's a French word.

"You know any Lithuanians?"

"No, Daddy-O. Just like the word 'Lithuania'. Man. Lithuania. Latvia. Estonia. All over the news, man. You know. The Baltic countries."

Fats finished and Joey put on another record and four vanilla-whites started singing. I tried not to crinkle my nose. I asked about Camp Records.

"John Livonius tried, man, he tried, but music's a hard business."

"Ever hear of Wanda Murphy?" I held up Lena's record. "She recorded this song for Camp Records in '40. Got some air time through the war."

He kept shaking his head. "Never carried much from Camp."

"Did you carry *any* of their records?"

Joey headed up the same aisle. "Still got one." He stopped, flipped through records. "Camp Records was a fly-by-night operation." He held up a record. "This one's a cover of a Little Walter number called *Hard Rain* sung by Sonny O'Malley." He took it to his record player, cut off the white singers, shaking his head at the record and he put it aside.

"That was *Tell Me Why* by the Four Aces. Pretty bad, huh, Daddy-O? They're white."

"I can tell."

"The voices?"

"Yeah, they're bad."

Joey put on *Hard Rain*. I heard raindrops falling as Joey stepped back over, said, "Lord save us from Rosemary Clooney, Doris Day and Perry Como."

When the song ended, I told Joey I'd take it as well. There were background singers on the song. Women. One could have been Wanda Murphy.

Joey put on another record, announcing *Bad, Bad Whiskey* by Amos Milburn and his Aladdin Chickenshackers. I walked out as bad, bad whiskey made the singer lose his happy home.

What the fuck was a chickenshacker?

A WOMAN SAT on the bench seat inside the foyer of our building. She stood up when I came in.

"Are you Mister Caye?"

"Depends."

She was in her forties, wore her blond hair back, away from her face, looked a little like Priscilla Lane in a clean, wholesome, way. Which is redundant. Pretty face. Big blue eyes. She wore an olive green dress and stood only about five-two.

"Depends?"

"Depends if you have a gun in that purse."

"Gun? Oh, my goodness no." She stepped close, extended her hand and said, "I believe you've been looking for me."

This was no blues singer.

"If you're Myrtle Littonel Slushy, then that's a Bingo."

"That I am and I did not kill my husband."

"You want to step into my office?"

"That's why I'm here."

I led the way in, waved to the desk for her to sit and stepped into the kitchen to start up a pot of coffee-and-chicory, telling her my secretary was off today, my maid as well, and my butler.

"You have all three?"

"That was a joke."

She waited for me to go around my desk to sit before she said, "Are you always this ... strange?"

"No." I tried to keep my face from expressing the fact this case was flat out batwing strange.

"Before we start." She put her purse up on the desk and pulled out a checkbook. "I want to hire you to clear my name."

"Your name's pretty clear at the moment. There's nothing to link you to your husband's murder except you were married to him."

She pulled out a ball point pen, opened the checkbook. "I was in Miami with the troupe when Sullivan was killed."

"What troupe?"

"Glendale Players of Metairie. Went out of business when the war ended."

"I suppose you could have hired someone. Who do you think killed your husband?"

She seemed to think a moment. "A burglar."

"According to the police report, there was no forced entry."

"A good burglar would leave no trace."

"A good burglar goes into a house to steal, not shoot someone in the back of the head."

She took in a deep breath. "Is five hundred enough for a retainer?"

I told her what I charge and she slid a check for five hundred across the wide desk to me.

"Now you're working for me." She sat up straighter and said, "My problem is I had a good motive. That's why I need your help."

"Motive?"

"Have you ever seen a picture of Sullivan?"

I shook my head and she pulled out a four-by-five inch picture from her purse and slid it across to me, telling me he was very handsome, looked a lot like Robert Taylor. "Wouldn't you say?"

"No."

He wasn't a bad looking fellow but I wouldn't describe Robert Taylor as particularly handsome either. Then again women see men differently.

"Sullivan was soft spoken with a deep, sensuous voice," her voice lower now, "and he was a cat chaser."

"A what?"

"Girls." She huffed at me. "Well, chaser isn't accurate. Females were drawn to him. That's how we met but I didn't know he liked young girls."

"How young?"

"He was fired from The Academy last year." She looked at the windows. "He impregnated more than one girl." She shook her head, looked back at me with glassy eyes. "He was so trusted he was the only male teacher allowed to chaperon the girls dormitory at night. Like letting a tom cat around kitties in heat. Apparently he was a night crawler, checking the girls at night. Eventually he came across one or two who were game."

"How did you find out?" If she told me Fanny, I was prepared to say this was way too easy.

"A man came to the house the Saturday before I left for Miami looking for Sullivan who was playing golf. He told me the whole sordid details of his daughter. I didn't get his name."

"You didn't think to mention this to the police?"

"They didn't ask me anything except where I was when Sullivan was killed." Her eyes were wet by now and she pulled out a handkerchief. "I was distraught."

Yeah. Of course.

"What did he look like?"

"Who?"

The grocery man. The milk man.

"The man who came by that Saturday."

I sat there and she gave me a pretty good description of Fanny Steele's father. A movement along the windows drew me to spot the orange tabby, the day shift tom cat, walking along the windowsill and looking in at us.

"So, you will take up my case?"

"Yes, ma'am." I asked for her address and phone number. She had an apartment in a very nice building on Saint Charles Avenue, just up from Carrollton. I'd been in the Herman Apartments just before the war, when I was a patrolman. An old man died in his sleep there.

I waited until she was about to get up to ask, "Why did you give Ernest Brienne's address as your forwarding address when you sold the house on Walnut Street?"

Her face reddened and a little smile came to her lips. "We've kept it secret which confirms why I made the right choice to hire you. You smoked out Ernest and me."

"Which brings me to my last question. What brought you to the lower Quarter? There are a lot of big shot PIs in the CBD."

"The newspapers, Mr. Caye. *The Item* referred to you as New Orleans's version of Philip Marlowe."

The reporter was poking fun at me.

"Marlowe's not real."

"He's as real as it gets with me. I've read the books and every story about him. Saw the movie five times."

The Big Sleep. Lord. How do I live up to that?

As soon as she left, I called Frenchy at home but no answer, so I sat behind my desk, put my feet up on it, my hands behind my head and closed my eyes. This was too easy. Mr. Steele showing up with the rare gun. Do these guys really think I don't know they're working together? What I hadn't figured out yet – is why did they come to me. Is it because police detectives would see right through this? I'll bet Mr. Steele has a better alibi than Myrtle. Was probably at dinner with the mayor or the DA. All I needed was Fanny coming in to tell me Sullivan was the father of her baby. And it occurred to me this big smoke screen was just that.

Hold Me, Babe

So who killed Sullivan Slushy? The betrayed wife? Her new boyfriend? The angry father? One of the impregnated women? Mother Superior for betraying The Academy? OK, that one was a stretch.

So I was back where I started.

Before going upstairs for supper with Jeannie, I checked the phone book on my other case, found seventeen O'Malleys in the phone book, none named Sonny.

IT WAS A thunderclap. I knew that when I woke with a jolt, my building shuddering with the sound wave. Only I saw sand and dirt rise in a bright sky before my eyes, felt it sting my face and I ducked as Field Marshal Kesselring's long range guns rained hell on the beach and ground around Anzio. I sat up in bed, head in my hands.

We should have been in Rome by then, but General Mark Clark hesitated, waited to solidify our position, allowed the wily German and his grenadier army to bring in the big guns. Patton wouldn't have hesitated. Hell, Stonewall Jackson wouldn't have hesitated. Even U.S. Grant would have kept pushing forward. You bloody the enemy, you keep pummeling him.

Lightning flashed outside and an even louder thunderclap crashed.

"Daddy. Daddy!"

I jumped out of bed and went into Jeannie's room as her kitten scrambled up on her bed and raced to her. Jeannie scooped it up and drew it to her face as I hesitated, glad I started wearing PJ bottoms to bed. I sat on the edge of the bed as more lightning danced outside and she crawled to me. I took her and the kitty in my arms.

"It's just a storm, baby."

She nodded and snuggled, climbed into my lap and I held her.

Too bad we couldn't stay that way. Her safe in my arms.

Eventually she fell asleep and I picked her up and brought her back around the bed, with her kitty still in her arms, and laid her down, pulled the sheet up, then went back to my bed and the flashbacks to that bloody fuckin' beach.

IT WAS A shot in the dark. We had an Irish Channel in New Orleans and O'Malley was as Irish as green beer. Hell, Murphy was an Irish name, not that I thought I'd find a black woman living between Magazine and Tchoupitoulas, Toledano down to First Street.

Settled by Irish immigrants in the early Nineteenth Century, they'd turned the area into their neighborhood. Starving Irish Catholics were brought in as expendable labor. They dug ditches, especially the New Basin Canal, until Yellow Fever ravaged them. These penniless families were misled to believe New Orleans was close to other Irish enclaves, New York and Boston. The Irish soon joined the stevedores, dock workers, saloon keepers and the New Orleans Police Department they dominated well into the Twentieth Century.

The place to start was Saint Alphonsus Catholic Church along narrow Constance Street in a neighborhood a step above mine. The brick houses were brown here, the wooden houses painted white with mostly dark green trim. I stood on the concrete banquette in front of Saint Alphonsus as a pigeon explored the recessed area outside the church's red door. The alcove with its three arches and narrow columns was made of cinder blocks painted white. Three towers topped by white crosses stood above the large church made of light brown brick.

Hold Me, Babe

I opened the door and stepped in, moved to the bastion of holy water, dipped my fingers in and made the sign of the cross, stood looking around the tall cathedral-like church. Two huge Greek columns, one with a huge crucifix attached stood up front and held up a roof painted with holy scenes. Below the crucifix was a statue of the Blessed Mother dressed in sky blue. The altar was adorned with gold paint and the coolest raised gazebo-like cubicle on the left where the priest delivered his sermon.

Three women in all black knelt in pews up front. I moved to the side and took the aisle up to an open doorway where priests usually dressed for mass, passing the Ways of The Cross and more statues of saints and the body of Christ. Dead Jesus lying on his back with the stigmata plainly visible and the statue of three saints hovering over him – Saint Joseph with baby Jesus, Mary in blue and a bishop-looking saint blessing the body. Beautiful statues actually.

I was hoping for Barry Fitzgerald or Bing Crosby. I found a brooding Mickey Rooney.

"What kinda name is Caye?" Father Callan examined my business card. "It's not Irish."

"French." Didn't think I should mention my mother was descended from Creole Spaniards as well.

Father Callan looked up at me with squinty eyes. He stood about five feet tall, a chubby man with a ruddy face and red hair. A Redemptorist priest, he wore a long black coat and black pants, a priest's white collar.

"Confessions start in a half hour," he told me.

"I'm not here for that, father. I'm looking for some people."

"From the way you ogled Mrs. Ennis when she passed outside, I think you need to go to confession."

Mrs. Ennis? On my way across the street I'd spied a blond in a green dress passing.

"I was just admiring her pumps, father."

He raised a finger at my chin. "You should not be admiring the breasts of married women."

"Pumps, father. Her shoes." I tried a smile. It didn't work.

He crossed his arms.

"I'm looking for a Sonny O'Malley."

"Sonny? You mean Lucius?"

"A singer, father. Recording artist."

He nodded. "Last I heard of Lucius, he went into the navy during the war. Haven't seen him since."

"Did he live around here? Any family?"

"His mother lived on Annunciation but she's dead."

I took a shot, asked about Wanda Murphy. The eyes grew more squinty. "Wanda should have gone to New York, L.A. Steered into mainstream music. They made her sound so Negro down here."

Wish I was better hiding my expressions.

"You're surprised?"

"That she's white? Yes."

"She *was*. I heard she finally left town during the war. Died in Idaho. Some God-forsaken place like that. No family as I can recall." He pulled at his collar. It looked too tight. "Wanda was not a good parishioner. Rarely went to mass."

I asked where she had lived and he hadn't a clue. He looked at his watch.

"I need to prepare for confessions."

"One more question, father. Ever hear of someone named Diluviennes?"

It was Father Callan's turn to fail hiding an expression. He shook his head.

"No" He stepped around me. "If that's all. I'll see you at confession."

You need to confess that last lie, father.

Diluviennes. It was in his eyes.

I DROPPED BY the Detective Bureau and not one detective was in. I left a message for Frenchy and headed to the library to hit the city directories again, checking out more years. Maybe I'd missed a Diluviennes. I hadn't. Found one O'Malley listed in the city directories on Annunciation Street from 1932 until 1947. E. O'Malley. I checked the French-English Dictionary and Annie Fordow was right. Diluviennes meant 'torrential' in French.

Back to the office, a calico cat scrambled across Barracks Street into the park as I pulled up and wondered if this was our kitten's mother. I timed it to be home when Jeannie got off the school bus so we could go straight to the vet.

The phone was ringing in my office. Edward Courant was on the line, asked if I'd made any progress.

"It might have helped if you'd told me Wanda Murphy was white." Actually, it wouldn't have but I just felt like saying that.

"I had no idea. I actually called to tell you I'd be out of town for the next three days."

I told him I was working on the case and we'd talk when he got back.

Had a little time so I called and re-checked all my contacts. Phone. Power. Gas. No Diluviennes. Ever.

JOHN STANFORD CAME out of his apartment as I unlocked the door to our apartment and Jeannie went in with the kitten.

"Boy or girl?"

"She's officially Harri with an 'I'. Why are you wearing an ascot? You expecting company?"

"If you don't wear things, they dry-rot on you. What? Ho?" John ran his fingers down the lapel of his maroon silk smoking jacket he wore today with green-and-blue tartan slacks and thick brown slippers. He followed me in and I put the large pizza box on the kitchen table and turned on the oven.

"Pizza?"

He crinkled his nose. "Never eat the stuff."

"You didn't eat filé gumbo until I introduced it to you."

"Yes, but I have tried pizza."

I reached into the cabinet and drew down a bottle of his favorite brew, Wells Bombardier Premium, popped open the cap and passed it to him. He stepped back into the living room as I slipped the pizza in the oven to warm it up.

Jeannie came rushing in from the bedroom carrying Harri on a pillow.

"She got her shots today. She's sleepy." Jeannie gently placed the pillow with her kitty on it on the sofa. "She's a mackerel cat."

"A what?" He looked at me.

"An American shorthair." I took out two plates and brought utensils to the table. "Alley cat. The vet says her coloring is classic mackerel tabby and white."

"Mackerel?"

"Gray and black stripping, unlike orange tabbies. He said to expect tan in her coat as she gets bigger."

John stepped back into the kitchen, whispered, "Is she old enough to get fixed?"

"In a few weeks."

Jeannie loved pepperoni pizza, especially the pepperoni. She ate one slice. I had three. When I put the leftovers in the fridge, all the pepperoni was gone. Cheese pizza in the fridge now.

THE MORNING PAPER had three articles on the front page about the war. After recapturing Seoul a couple weeks ago, General MacArthur now threatened to carry the war all the way to the Chinese border. Again. We were just up there before the Chinese sent in about a million troops. B-29s were bombarding Chinese supply routes in Korea, maybe across the Yalu River. He's bombing China?

President Truman keeps calling it a police action, rather than a war, and it's a 'UN-mandated Action'. Yeah? Nearly 90% of the troops fighting the communists were American. Fuck. Who gives a damn what kind of government runs that frozen tundra? Apparently we do. Fuckin' 'Domino Theory'. If we don't hold the line in Korea and Indochina, communists will over-run the planet, like locusts. I'd seen enough propaganda from WWII to recognize it when I saw it.

Didn't learn from the Nazis, did we? As soon as ole Winston Churchill called it the Iron Curtain, we saw communists as inhuman and we all saw what the Nazis did to people they thought were not human.

I had my feet up on my desk when my door opened and Fanny stepped in wearing a purple ball gown. Well, it looked like a ball gown.

"I came to warn you."

"That your father's going to shoot me." I pulled my feet down.

She almost jumped in place. "Yes." She looked around as she came in slowly, frilly slip making scratching noises, "Did he come by already?"

"Yep." I waited for her to get close before adding, "He brought a gun."

She put a hand over her mouth.

"I took it away from him, instead of shooting the fool."

She came and sat heavily in a chair in front of my desk.

"Who told him about me?"

She looked confused. She hadn't rehearsed that I may ask that particular question, apparently.

"I uh, I think. Angél must have told him."

I scooped up my phone's receiver and called the Brienne house. Mary answered and brought Angél to the phone.

"It's me, Lucien." I watched Fanny as I spoke. "Have you spoken with Fanny's father the last few days?"

"Fanny's father? I haven't seen him in months."

"So you didn't give him my name."

"Goodness, no."

"What about your father? You told your father about me?"

Sometimes a pause tells you a lot.

"Um. I uh, had to mention you when he asked about your car in the driveway."

"Thanks." I hung up. Fanny's face looked paler now.

"It wasn't Angél. Was it you?"

"No."

"That only leaves Angél's father."

"Or Myrtle." She bit her lower lip right away.

I picked up my t-ball jotter, flicked it to expose the pen's tip, flicked it again. "When was the last time you spoke to Myrtle."

"I ... uh. Uh. Never have."

I scooped up the phone again. "I should have asked Angél if her father's in." I started to dial. "You know if he's at home or at Myrtle's?"

"I don't have the Herman number."

I huffed, hung up the receiver. *She knows about the Herman Apartments.*

"OK. Let's go over this again."

Fanny took in a deep breath, sat up straighter and said, "I haven't seen my father like this in a long time."

"Since when?"

"Since I got pregnant."

I watched her eyes. "Did Sullivan Slushy have anything to do with that?"

She looked at the windows. "I thought so at first but once my baby was born I saw the resemblance to another boy I knew." She took in a deep breath. "A simple blood test proved Sullivan wasn't the father."

"Who was this other boy?"

She shook her head. "He was killed on Saipan."

"Does your father know about you and Sullivan?"

"He suspected when Sullivan was fired. He thinks he put two-and-two together."

"You think he shot Sullivan?"

"Oh, my goodness no. We were together in Shreveport at a War Bond Rally with big bosses from Shell Oil, Mayor Masteri and Governor Jones." She leaned forward. "They didn't like each other one bit."

When she left, I felt little crawly things on my arms.

Give me a good suspect with what could be the murder weapon – then give me his alibi.

Someone was leading me around by the nose.

THE COLD HALLS of Orleans Parish Prison smelled of pine oil and urine. I could only imagine what the cells smelled like in this cement hulk attached to the rear of the Criminal Courts Building. My eyes were beginning to water from the stench before a guard led me into what the police use as an interview room. It didn't stink in there, or maybe my nostrils were used to it.

I sat at the small table and they brought an emaciated man who could be from fifty to seventy years old. In prison denims, he stood about five-eight, weighed maybe one-twenty with gray-white hair hanging long and straight. He shivered as he sat, asked me for a cigarette.

"Hello, Sonny."

I pulled out three packs of Chesterfields, an Almond Joy, a Mounds and a Milky Way candy bar. "Found an old lady on Annunciation Street who said you were probably here." I looked at the walls. "Spend a lot of time here, don't you?"

In the drunk tank.

Bleary eyes stared back at me. "They'll send me back to the hospital. I get cleaned out for a while."

I passed him the cigarettes and candy bars and a business card. "I'm looking for someone who sang with you at Camp Records."

He nodded, shaking as he reached for the goodies.

"Wanda Murphy."

He picked up the Almond Joy. Sniffed it.

"She's in a Canal Cemetery."

"Sure about that? I heard she went to Idaho."

"Who the hell goes to Idaho?" He shook his head. "I went to her funeral. Saint Patrick's Cemetery, I think. On Canal."

"Her song – "

"How Could You Leave Me. Shoulda been a hit. Fuckin' Camp Records didn't know squat."

"Do you know who wrote it?"

He shook his head.

"The name's listed as A. Diluviennes."

He started coughing and I stood up, moved as far away as I could as he hacked up something from a lung, spat it into the trash can next to the table. He wiped his mouth with his shirt sleeve.

"Wanda have any family you know of?"

"Had a daughter. Alice. I think."

The coughing started up again. Worse this time. I waited for him to recover to ask if he thought of anything else. I pointed to my card and stepped to the door.

"No matches?"

I pulled a couple packs of matches from my other coat pocket, put them on the table. "Didn't want you blowing smoke in my face."

I slipped the head guard a fiver.

"I don't take bribes."

"It's not a bribe. It's a tip. I believe in tipping. Don't you?"

JEANNIE HAD A message for me when I got home. She raced to the phone and picked up the small notepad I kept next to the phone. Harri ran to her food dish, saw there was only a little left from her morning feed and went, "Meow."

"Mister Frenchy called." She held up the pad and read it aloud. "I wrote exactly what he said. 'Wrong gun, Pretty Baby." She smiled at me. "What does that mean?"

"It means Daddy's got more work to do. A lot more."

"I mean, why does he call you 'Pretty Baby'?"

"Because he's a crazy man and thinks it's funny."

"If he thinks you're pretty, he's wrong. Men aren't pretty. They are handsome. Like you." She tapped her foot. "I'll have to tell Mr. Frenchy he's saying it wrong."

"Yeah. Good luck."

Harri decided climbing up my pants leg was a good idea, looking up at me and going, "Rowl. Rowl." She let out a long meow, sounding like she was starving to death. I pulled her off, her claws digging into my hands, handed her to Jeannie.

Whatever was in the pot simmering on the stove smelled wonderful. As I went to it, Jeannie said Kaye made us red beans. I lifted the lid and sure enough, a huge pot of red beans.

"She breaded the pork chops," Jeannie said. "They're in the fridge."

I told her she could help with the rice while I started up the chops, but only after we fed the starving, little furry girl.

FATHER CALLAN STOOD in front of his church with arms folded and looking around, most likely watching for men checking out the breasts of married women. I parked right across from him, climbed out of my Ford. I left my coat in the car. Let him see my .357 magnum revolver in the holster on my hip.

He didn't notice me until I was almost on him. I moved straight up, close, too close, looked down in his chubby face. I planned to tell him off, but two passing women stopped to watch and this was a priest after all. I took a step back.

"Father, Wanda Murphy's buried here in town. You knew that didn't you?"

He looked up with that English bulldog face. Said nothing.

"I heard she's buried in Saint Patrick's. If so, she was passed through church. Your church?"

"No."

I nodded slowly. "OK. Now tell me again the name Diluviennes means nothing to you."

He looked over his shoulder and I followed him into the recessed area by the front door of his church.

Hold Me, Babe

"A big man came around last night looking for Wanda's daughter. He tried giving me the nice treatment but he was slimy and I think he was a gangster. Mafia maybe. He looked Italian."

I pulled out a small notepad and pen, asked for a description of the man, wrote it down – 5'9", 280 pounds, balding, big moustache, wore a rumpled suit, drove a pre-war Cadillac. Black.

"He leave a name?"

"No."

"How old is this daughter?"

"I only saw her a couple times. Years ago. Redheaded little girl. She's probably twenty now. Thereabouts. Name was Alice or something like that."

"Her father?"

He shook his head. "Saw her with her mother at Saint Patrick's Day Parades."

"If you didn't pass Wanda through church, how'd she get into a Catholic cemetery."

"Who says she did?"

A stone fuckin' drunk.

NEXT STOP WAS the Office of the Archdiocese next to Notre Dame Seminary, Carrollton Avenue and Walmsley where I found a baptism record from December 28, 1925, for a female child Alizée Marie Diluviennes, born November 17, 1925, to mother Wanda Kathleen Murphy and father André Louis Diluviennes, a citizen of France. The daughter was now twenty-five. Baptism information did not include addresses. She was baptized by Archbishop Shaw at Saint Louis Cathedral.

Father was André Diluviennes, citizen of France. A. Diluviennes? Was this my songwriter?

I might be getting close with this case.

MYRTLE SLUSHY CLAIMED she was in Miami with the Glendale Players of Metairie the night her husband was murdered. With no listing in the phone book, I got to the library when it opened – I'm a freaking library detective on these cases – and found them in the 1943 suburban directory. No listing in 1944. Address was 118 Metairie Road, which turned out to be a One Hour Martinizing Cleaners.

"Previous tenants?" I asked a sweaty cleaner.

"Who?"

I learned who owned the building and it was the archdiocese of New Orleans. This property was administered by the monsignor at nearby Saint Francis Xavier Church. Of course, the monsignor wasn't in but a chatty, busy-body church secretary had worked across the street from the Glendale Players and was positive they went out of business at the end of 1943. Positive.

THE DIRECTORY OF Saint Patrick's Cemeteries on Canal Street had no listing for a Wanda Murphy or any Diluviennes. I had to park over by Odd Fellow's Rest. No way Wanda was buried in Odd Fellow's. It was for foreign seamen.

I spied one of the attendants at Cypress Grove across Canal Street as he stood smoking a cigarette just outside that cemetery. I waited for a streetcar to pass, crossed Canal and went up to him. He towered over me, standing about six-five, weighing a good two eighty with coal black skin and wearing a white shirt and khaki slacks. This wasn't one of the grave workers.

"You work in Cypress Grove?"

Hold Me, Babe

"Yes, sir. I'm the assistant attendant. Mr. Water's off today."

"I'd like to check the directory."

He tossed the cigarette away. "Well, come on in." He led me to the small building just within the tall wrought iron gates. There were two desks inside, several chairs and filing cabinets. He stepped to a card cabinet and I gave him the name Wanda Murphy. He found it in less than a minute.

"Buried here on January 19, 1944. She's in back, in the wall. Second tier, number 767, just past the last big oak tree."

I had my notebook out and wrote it down. "Who's paying for the perpetual care?"

I paid ten dollars a year to Saint Roch Cemetery for my parents' tomb. Perpetual care kept the tomb clean.

"I can't give out that information." He came and sat at the desk in front of where I stood.

I looked at the name tag on his overall, nodded, took out a business card and a ten dollar bill. I put both on the desk.

"Sammy. There's a girl who may be in danger. I'm not a thug and I ain't the police. I'm the good guy you go to when you can't go to the cops. Please. I need your help."

He twisted his head to the side.

"I could lose my job."

I looked out at the marble sepulchres, concrete tombs of this above-ground cemetery, what we call a 'little city of the dead' here in New Orleans. I slipped my notepad back in to my coat pocket, pointed to the back of the cemetery.

"All the way," he said. There was a softness in his eyes now, but his mouth was still shut.

It was a hike, well over a hundred yards. Unlike most of our cemeteries, Cypress Grove had many trees, large ones, live oaks and magnolias, even a few towering pecan trees. The walls on either side were lined with walled tombs like ovens where caskets were slipped in. Some of the masonry had fallen away from the bricks and the marker of Wanda's tomb. Moss covered her name, chiseled in block letters along with her dates of birth and death.

A blue jay fussed at me as I moved back past an oak tree. They were known to dive bomb people as well, but this one was content to fuss only. I looked up at an airplane high above, heading out of town from Moisant Field.

Sammy stood by the gate with his arms folded. I waved to him and started to walk by and he nodded me over.

"I had to write it down, the name has a lot of letters." He slipped me a scrap of paper. I thanked him.

I waited to look after I got into the Ford. He'd written: Diluvines 1018 Julia St. He'd missed some letters in the last name.

THE BUILDING WAS an old, narrow brownstone in the Central Business District. Three stories but only about twenty yards wide. Sandwiched between two new buildings, it had to be a Nineteenth Century leftover with a gas lamp perpetually lit next to his tall front door of heavy cypress. A small brass plaque read: Varenne Maritime Law. The door was locked so I rang the bell, heard it chime. After the third ring a small porthole opened in the door and part of a face peeked out at me through iron bars.

I took a step back and said, "I'm a private investigator." I held up my business card. "May I come in and speak with someone?"

"What about?"

"A girl named Alice."

I heard voices whispering before the porthole clamped shut. I thought it was a brush off until the door creaked opened to a semi-dark foyer. I stepped in, smelling lemon oil, saw the floor was a little dusty. Two old men stood next to one another to my left, both in black suits, both with pallid white faces. One smiling, the other grimacing.

"I am Joseph Varenne," said smiley face, "and my brother is Crabby Varenne."

Crabby shoved his brother's shoulder and said he was Craig Varenne.

I introduced myself and passed each a card.

"We are on our way out," Joseph said as the two examined my card in the dim light.

"What do you want?" said Crabby.

"Is there an Alice here?"

"No."

Joseph looked up at me. I say *up* because these two men were shorter than Father Callan. I watched their eyes.

"What about an Alizée?"

Typically lawyers are better at keeping their faces from revealing anything but Joseph had lost the touch. He shook his head but I knew better.

"Does the name Diluviennes mean anything to y'all?"

Joseph looked at my card again and Crabby glared at me, said, "No."

"You guys have a secretary?"

"Mrs. Benton left early but her first name's not Alice or that other name."

I thanked them and stepped back out to a dark-clouded sky. As I pulled away, I spotted two good surveillance positions for future reference.

I BEAT THE rainstorm home, thinking about my other case, realizing this Slushy matter was a case of purposeful deception. No way a suspect hires me to prove she didn't commit a murder and gives me an alibi so easy to disprove.

It's like I'm stuck in a bad play without the script. Everyone knows their lines except me.

I ate a late lunch, a nice thick ham and cheese sandwich with potato chips and a Coke. The heavy rain slackened as I waited with Harri for Jeannie to get home from school.

Lethargy dragged me to the sofa and stretched me out and Harri climbed on me and off, nibbling my fingers, finally settled between my feet. I'd taken off my shoes and I'm sure my socks were warm. My eyes closed and I let myself drift back a year, no, not quite a year and Callie Colwyn's blue eyes were there, her lovely face moving close, crimson lips pursed ready to kiss me. And I go there, remember that sleek naked body, full breasts and the French kisses.

She left me for a rich guy.

Women have been walking in and out of my life since high school. Like Jeannie's mother. I'd only dated her a few times back in '42. Jane Levant was a waitress and I was a cop who went off to war. She wrote me when I was in boot camp but when I shipped out for Ranger training in Scotland, she quit writing. The last night I spent with Jane was in July '42. We thought we'd been careful with the sex. She called it the 'rhythm method', something about a woman recognizing the days she's fertile and not having sex before and during those days. Didn't work and Jeannie was born April 15, 1943. Didn't even know I had a daughter until her mother dropped her off at my doorstep, on her way out of town.

Harri came up and lay next to my neck and we fell asleep. Good little girl.

Nice way to spend a rainy afternoon.

THE DOORBELL WOKE us and Harri scrambled off me and off the sofa. I looked at the clock. Ten minutes after two and the rain had slowed. A little. I hit the buzzer, went out to

Hold Me, Babe

the landing to see who I'd buzzed in, making sure our escape-artist kitten hadn't followed me out of the apartment.

A man with a large black umbrella stepped in, moved it aside and there was a girl with him. He looked up and it was my NOPD buddy Kirk Eckland in civvies. He grinned at me. The girl's dark hair was drenched and she looked up as well, blinked at me. She looked like a teen-ager. I waved them up, met them at my apartment door with a couple towels.

Eckland stood my height, a smidge over six feet. His dark hair was wiry, while mine was straight, and he was a little heavier but he had a quick smile. He passed a towel to the girl whose chin was down so I couldn't see her clearly. She rubbed the towel through her long hair while he wiped off his arms.

"We tried walking the last blocks," he said. "Damn rain swept across us."

The girl stood about five-six. She wore a plain tan dress, A-line. I still read the fashion page of the *Eagle* so I knew what an A-line dress was like. This one seemed a size too large. She was petite and when she threw her hair back it glistened reddish-brown. Auburn. She still didn't meet my eyes and she was soaked.

"Get in here," I told them, made sure Harri didn't escape and closed the door. I went straight into the bathroom and lit the gas heater, came out and pointed over my shoulder and told her there was a terry cloth robe hanging behind the bathroom door. "Go in and dry off."

I went into the kitchen to start up a fresh pot of coffee-and-chicory. Eckland stepped in, rubbing the towel over his clothes.

"You have a kitten?"

I looked back and Harri stood up on the sofa, watching us.

"How is Jeannie getting along in school?"

"Well. Very well. Better than I ever did in school."

He sat at the table, nodded toward my bedroom and the bathroom. "Alice asked me to bring her here."

"Here?" I sat across from him.

"To see you."

"Yeah?"

"Said you were looking for her. Asked if I knew you." He leaned back. "I handled a 103 at her boarding house few months ago and her ex-boyfriend made the classic mistake. Tried to fight the police. He went to Charity before jail and ain't been back since."

She stepped back into the living room and headed our way. In my robe and slippers, the robe way too long and wrapped tightly around her, she spied Harri and waved to the kitty before moving to us.

I stood as she stopped and looked at me with doe-eyes, wide, the color of dark chocolate. I had no clue what her eyes were telling mine but our eyes communicated something on an elemental level that drew my breath slowly out and left me just standing there. It took a few moments to see a fearful innocence in her eyes, a lot like that sweet look Jeannie gave me the first time I saw her standing outside my building with her suitcase.

"You two all right?"

I nodded.

"Alice, this is Lucien Caye, Private Eye. Lucien, meet Alice."

I shook my head, smiled, said, "It isn't Alice. It's Alizée. A French name. Alizée Diluviennes, which means 'torrential' in French. I looked it up."

I sat back down and she came to sit at the table. She wore little make-up, if any, except a hint of red lipstick and looked more like an eighteen year old than twenty-five. Her nose was slightly upturned. She was strikingly pretty. Not like the chic women I usually dated but a muted beauty, almost hidden by shyness. Her dark auburn hair, hanging damp on the towel draped across her shoulder, was redder than Callie's and much longer.

"Most people call me Alice," she said.

"I'm not most people."

Kirk knuckled my shoulder.

"Mr. Varenne said you were looking for me," she said.

"Joe or Crabby?"

She stiffened a moment then her lips almost curled into a smile.

"Mr. Joseph."

"Fix the coffees," I told Eckland and went out into the living room. The rain outside had stopped. Harri followed me to the Philco. I scooped her up and saw the record was still on the player so I turned it on, came back as the whispering began on the song. Alizée had twisted around in the chair and I stopped and leaned against the end of my sofa, petting the kitty.

Wanda Murphy's sad voice filled the room and the words bounced off me as her daughter's eyes grew damp –

> How could you leave our love?
> How could you leave me?
> How could you leave our world,
> and the nights we set afire?
> Our nights, Babe. Our streets, Babe
> Marigny. Frenchmen. Piety and Desire

Tears came when her mother's voice broke over the lines – "Come back and touch me, Babe. Hold me, Babe."

Eckland laid out three cups of coffee, cream and sugar and I saw him sit, start fixing his cup as the song ended.

I put Harri on the sofa, stepped back to the table.

"Did your father write this song?"

She shook her head, lips quivering now. She wiped her eyes, took in a breath, said, "I wrote it."

My knees felt a little rubbery so I sat.

"You? You were what, fifteen, when this song was recorded."

She dabbed her eyes with the towel. Reached for the cream and sugar.

"I was fourteen when I wrote *Hold Me, Babe.* They changed the title."

Eckland gave me the look a dog gives when someone makes a strange sound.

"When my Papa left, my Mama stayed up nights crying. Drinking. She mumbled things. She said some of the things in the song and I felt – " Alizée's voice cracked. "He left me too."

She took in a deep breath, raising a shaky coffee cup to her lips.

The apartment door opened and John brought Jeannie in. He liked meeting Jeannie at the bus stop, which was right at the corner.

Jeannie scooped Harri from atop the sofa and dropped her school bag, turned and said, "Hello, Mr. Kirk."

I introduced Alizée and Jeannie came over and shook her hand.

"Did you meet Harri with an 'I'? She's a girl."

Alizée pet Harri's head and the kitten swatted at her.

John joined us for a cup of coffee, the old boy eyeing Alizée in the robe. He never missed a pretty girl. Eckland got up, went over to the Philco and started the song back up again.

Jeannie said, "My Daddy plays that song a lot. I think it's sad."

Alizée almost smiled.

It supposed to be sad, darling.

I took a sip of coffee and she did as well as Jeannie went out to the sofa to pick up one of Harri's ribbons to get the kitty worked up. The song played and when it ended Eckland looked back at the kitchen.

"You wrote this when you were fourteen?"

Her big eyes were on mine again. "Yes."

Eckland stopped to pet Harri on his way to the kitchen.

"The whispering at the beginning?" I leaned closer to Alizée as tears welled in her eyes again.

"That's me." She smiled slightly, wiping the tears away. "Telling my mama not to cry when she sings the song. You have the original recording here. Camp Records released a second take and you don't hear my whispering. My mama's voice broke in that one too. So why are you looking for me?"

Eckland joined us at the table.

I slapped my forehead. "I have good news for you, young lady. Your song was used in an Orson Welles movie and you have money coming to you from royalties. And Lena Horne just released your song and there will be more royalty money for the songwriter. You can prove your wrote it, I hope."

She nodded. "I copyrighted it, just like all my other songs and registered them with ASCAP."

Eckland cut in. "Other songs?"

"Twenty-six others." Her voice came stronger now.

I told her about Edward Courant and how he'd be out of town a few days but as soon as he came back I'd take her to him.

"What about the other man looking for me?"

"Father Callan told you?" The priest who never heard the name Diluviennes.

"Oh, yes."

I explained about the fat man to Eckland.

"What could that be about?"

Everyone looked at me, even Harri. I suggested we start thinking about supper.

JOHN HAD PLANS, so did Kirk Eckland. Alizée sat with Jeannie and Harri and I warned them to buzz no one into the building and keep the apartment door locked. Anything suspicious, call the police right away.

I gave them the choice and they chose burgers and fat steak fries from the Clover Grill. I called ahead and checked the Ford's engine, as I always did now, for any of Harri's kin. I drove around the block before leaving, looking for a black Cadillac or a fat man.

Alizée's hair was finally dry and had a slight wave as we sat around the table eating. Harri seemed content to stand in Jeannie's lap, paws up on the table and just watch.

"What's your connection with the Varenne brothers?"

"I work there. I'm their secretary."

"Who's Mrs. Benton?"

"She's also their secretary but she's getting too old to do the heavy typing, filing motions, court papers, going to the court house."

I took a bite of burger, asked with a full mouth. "How old are these people?"

Alizée shrugged. "Mrs. Benton uses a cane to get around and the brothers had dinner once with George Washington."

"Really?" Jeannie said.

Hold Me, Babe

Alizée laughed and her face really lit up. Harri took her shot, jumped on the table and bit into the meat hanging out the side of Jeannie's burger before we could move. The little thing growled when Jeannie pulled her away.

I broke off a piece of my burger and gave it to Harri.

"Daddy! You told me to never give her table food."

"I got to get on her good side, don't I?"

I told our guest I was a pretty bad father and regretted it immediately as she went sullen again.

"You're not bad," Jeannie said. "You're just a big juvenile delinquent sometimes."

Glad I'd just swallowed.

"Where'd you hear that term?"

What a dumb question.

Jeannie and Alizée both answered, "School."

HER DRESS WAS still a little damp but she couldn't go home in my robe. Alizée Marie Diluviennes lived in a boarding house run by a WWI widow named Mrs. Woodruff, a three story Creole townhouse, two buildings up from Toulouse on Burgundy Street, nine blocks from my building.

"I'm only a block from the streetcar line." She meant Rampart Street.

I hadn't noticed her perfume until we were in the car. It was light. A fragrance unfamiliar to me. I made sure I had her phone numbers – home and work and she had mine.

"Jeannie wants to see *Alice in Wonderland*," Alizée told me as she toyed with the hem of her dress, much like I've seen Jeannie do. Her eyes were like black agates staring back at me. She added, "There's an advanced showing this Sunday. A matinee."

Had to stop in the street with no parking spots open and she climbed out, came around to my side of the car.

"She just mentioned out of the blue she wanted to see the movie?" Wish my daughter would tell me things like that.

The lights of a car coming down Burgundy closed on us.

"She was a little afraid when you went to get supper, so I recited *Jabberwocky* to her. She'd never heard it."

"Jabber who?"

Alizée put a hand on my car, fist on her hip, said, "Twas brillig, and the slithy toves did gyre and gimble in the wabe."

The car behind blew its horn when it stopped.

"What was that?"

She took her hand down and stepped away.

"All mimsey were the borogoves, and the mome raths outgrabe."

Driver behind leaned on the horn.

She laughed, backed away. "That's Lewis Carroll. Man who wrote *Alice in Wonderland*."

"That's English?"

The horn stopped and the driver stuck his head out of his car. "Pay the whore and get outta my way!" He leaned on the horn again.

I climbed out and nodded for Alizée to go inside. She stepped to her doorway and I went to the car behind me, a '47 Chevy coupe in an ugly-ass purple color. The driver, a man, rolled up his window as I stepped up. I ripped off his side-view mirror, tossed it on his hood and went back to my car.

Alizée stood in the doorway of her building and slowly waved at me as I drove off, thinking again how she was twenty-five and not a teen-ager. I was only six years older than her.

I BEAT THE rain home and Jeannie was in her pajamas on the sofa.

"*Ella and the Pirates* in ten minutes."

I pulled Harri off the wall and handed her to my daughter. How a kitten was able to climb up wood paneling was beyond me. I scooped up the paper, flipped to the amusements, found the ad for *Alice in Wonderland*. I picked up the phone and dialed the number to the boarding house.

An old woman answered and I asked for Alizée.

"You the man who dropped her off?"

"Yes, ma'am."

"Wish you would have punched the asshole in the jaw. Hold on a minute. I'll get Alice."

When she came on I asked why people called her Alice.

"It's easier."

"The matinee is noon Sunday at the Saenger. We can pick you up around eleven fifteen, OK?"

She let out a breath, came back with, "Is this a date, Lucien?"

"You bet. You'll be safe. Jeannie will chaperone."

"Sounds like a good plan."

I thought a moment, then said, "This was your plan all along wasn't it?"

"I was worried when you didn't ask right away. I can see I have my work cut out with you, don't I?" She sounded a little older on the phone, more like a woman, twenty instead of eighteen.

"Dad. Dad. Dad. The radio."

"I have to go now. Ella found a baby tyrannosaurus and Owen wants to raise it to sic on the pirates."

"What?"

"*Ella and the Pirates*. CBS radio. Coming on now and I have to listen."

"When you tore off that mirror, I thought. Yep. A juvenile delinquent." She laughed.

AT MIDNIGHT, I popped a Falstaff and lay on my sofa, misty air flowing through the open dormers atop the balcony doors. It smelled like rain again and in the distant sky I spied forks of lightning. The showers of late spring in New Orleans.

It had been a good day, finding Alizée. Hope she was getting a load of money. I liked the way she clicked with Jeannie and liked the way she looked at me, has her work cut out with me. She was a diamond in the rough, prettier than she realized. She was also a conundrum – yes, they taught us a few big words at Holy Cross. A girl who could write a heart-wrenching torch song at fourteen and looked eighteen eleven years later.

I liked the way she brought up the movie.

What was that jabber thing she was talking about?

It wasn't until I was in bed and drifting off did my mind move to the other case and I thought – *puppet-master.*

Someone was pulling strings in my other case.

Who?

Had to be Mister Ernest Brienne. Super rich pillar of society. Why? In my drowsiness, my brain tried to tell me it had something to do with the girlfriend, Myrtle. In my half-sleep I saw them as marionettes loosened by Brienne.

Fanny's father and the gun. Probably thought I'd drag the old man to the cops before I checked out the Harlow. Muddy the water some more. Angél and Fanny coming to me. Myrtle too. Brienne. It had to be him.

I wondered, as I slipped away, if he was a good poker player.

THE ROLLS ROYCE drove leisurely from Audubon Place down to the CBD and into the Baronne Building garage. I parked at a meter on the street and went in, told the elevator operator the twelfth floor and he asked, "Do you have an appointment?"

I handed him a business card. He took it and asked who I was looking for on the twelfth floor.

"Ernest Brienne."

He pulled a pair of glasses from his maroon jacket, looked at a notepad on a small table beneath the elevator buttons.

"I don't see your name listed."

"Call up."

He shrugged, picked up the elevator phone, dialed and waited. I pegged him to be in his mid sixties. His uniform hung loosely and those eyes had a drinker's gleam. Thankfully elevators just went *up* and *down*.

"I have a Mr. Caye here, C A Y E, for Mr. Brienne," he said into the receiver, looked at my card again, added, "Lucien Caye. He's some sort of investigator."

He covered the mouthpiece, told me they were checking.

I could smell it now, beer and cigarettes. I eased into the far corner and he said into the phone, "Yes, ma'am."

We went straight up and the elevator opened to a reception area where a woman too young to be wearing horn-rimmed glasses asked me to wait a moment, pointing to a plush tan sofa where I sat and waited. She returned to her typing and I don't remember seeing anyone type so fast before. A light drizzle tapped against the windows next to me and with the pitter-patter of typing, my eyes grew heavy and I fought to keep from nodding off as the minutes ticked away.

She had to shake my arm to wake me and I saw I'd been out nearly forty-five minutes. She giggled and said Mr. Brienne will see me now. She wore a black dress. On her way back to her desk, she pointed to a tall set of double doors to my right. I yawned, stretched and realized the room smelled of citrus. Furniture polish no doubt.

I stepped through the double door to an office that had to be fifty yards long with plush dark green carpeting, no furniture for thirty yards, just a long row of windows on the left overlooking the city skyline and a line of fine art prints in massive frames on the right. Monet, Van Gogh, Rembrandt, some nudes of women lying casually in forests with little angels, deer, rabbits munching greenery around them.

Ernest Brienne, hands flat on his massive mahogany desk, had a tycoon look with thick, wavy black hair, deep set brown eyes and wearing a dark red tie with his white shirt. He waved to the large, maroon cushioned chairs in front of his desk. I sat in the one on the left and realized I might need a crane to get out of the soft chair.

Brienne gave me a well-practiced smile. "You saved me the trouble of going to the Lower Quarter to see you."

I shrugged.

"If you had children, Mr. Caye, you'd understand what I'm about to tell you."

Knows about the Lower Quarter, but not everything about me.

"Well, it isn't easy bringing them up these days. Especially girls." He leaned back. "I don't even try to control my daughter or girlfriend. A man who tries to do such a silly thing with women is a fool.

"So when they spend money to have someone like you look into a matter, I'm not concerned. That my daughter dislikes my girlfriend enough to accuse her of murder bothers me even less because I know Myrtle killed no one."

He reached into a desk drawer and pulled out a large envelope, slid it to me.

Hold Me, Babe

"Myrtle wasn't in Miami. She was with me in Aspen, Colorado." He nodded to the envelope and I opened it to a brochure of a ski resort, room receipts and a series of photos of Brienne and Myrtle around the resort and on skis.

"Joshua Steele wants his pistol back. You can drop it off here tomorrow."

"It's being compared to bullets from unsolved crimes. Homicides, robberies. It'll take a while."

"It's at NOPD? Never mind. My attorneys will get it back from them. Keep the retainers, Mr. Caye. You can notify my daughter and my girlfriend over the phone that your investigation is over. There's no rush."

He passed a business card to me. "My private number's at the bottom. So you won't waste time sitting in my waiting room. Did you have a nice nap?"

I SNATCHED UP the phone after the first ring. It was Father Callan.

"Two other men came by looking for Wanda's daughter. I think they're gangsters."

"I'll be right there."

He was waiting for me outside with two women in print dresses, flat shoes, looked like housewives who stepped away before I stepped up, both lowering their eyes so I couldn't see them. The good priest probably alerted them to my unsavory reputation.

"They had heavy accents."

"Those two?" I nodded to the retreating women.

"The gangsters." Damn he looked so much like a pissed-off Mickey Rooney, I had to look away from his scowl.

"With heavy accents."

"What kind of accent?"

"Foreign."

"Italian? French? German?"

He opened his arms, hands palms up.

"Did they sound like Louis Prima? Maurice Chevalier? Or Hitler?"

"Hitler? No!"

His face scrunched up. "French, I think. But not smooth like Charles Boyer. Rougher. Only one spoke and he growled."

I took out my notepad and pen, asked what the men looked like, wrote – #1 5'6", heavy set, scar on left cheek, thick moustache, wore a turtle neck shirt and black pants – #2, heavy set, looked bigger, had a moustache too, stayed in car – green Chevy or Olds. Both were dark-skinned.

"Olive skinned," Father Callan said. "Looking more like Portuguese than Frenchmen." He shoved my arm. "Maybe they were Portuguese."

"What did they say, exactly?"

The heavy set man with the moustache climbed out of the Chevy when the priest stepped out of church early that morning and asked for the daughter of Wanda Murphy, was not happy with Father Callan's answer and warned the priest they would be back and expected a better answer.

"If they come back, call the police right away and get their license plate, Father. Then call me."

"That's it? That's all you're going to do."

I put the notepad back into my coat pocket.

"Did they know her name?"

"No."

"Did the fat man the other day mention her name?"

"Now that I think about it. No."

"Good."

I left him there, still glowering at me.

EDWARD COURANT PASSED the birth certificate, driver's license and copyright registration paper back to Alizée Marie Diluviennes, then dug into his brown leather briefcase. They sat in the chairs in front of my desk, while I sat in the captain's chair behind.

The old man wore a dark blue suit, this one recently pressed. His eyebrows still looked like chubby caterpillars and his white hair still frizzed ala-Albert Einstein. Alizée wore a blue and white striped sundress with a light white jacket, white heels, her hair pinned up with barrettes on either side. She was too pretty to be described as cute and I could see, hidden maybe on purpose, a knockout, a stone-gorgeous woman.

"I am so sorry that your mother is not here for this." Courant pulled a file from his briefcase. "I am amazed, however, that you wrote such a passionate song at such a young age, but Mozart wrote his first opera at a tender age. I'm not saying you are a genius like Mozart. I'm just saying music is a wonder and knows no age constraints."

Courant withdrew three envelopes from the file, pulled papers and a check from each.

"From Mercury Productions, here is a check from the standard percentage of music royalty for use of your song in the movie."

Alizée looked at the check, then at me with wide eyes.

"If the movie is sold to television, which is likely, then you will receive more money from whatever network purchases the film."

He passed a second check and royalty statement. "This money was earmarked for you via Camp Records, but they are defunct, happens often, so ASCAP kept your royalties in escrow. Their address is on the statement. Contact them so they know where to send future royalties."

He gave her the last document and check. "From Duchess Records, here is a royalty agreement where you will receive your standard royalty from Lena Horne's cover of your song, which is a hit. The check includes your first royalties."

Alizée blinked at each check, back and forth.

"As soon as I confirm your mother is deceased, I'll make sure you receive any money coming to her. If there are any other relatives, you can share it."

Courant closed his briefcase, looked at me. "Good work. I must say I was surprised you found her." He waited for Alizée to look at him again. "Mr. Caye tells me you've written more songs." He handed her a business card. "I manage talent, among my many endeavors and I may not look like a player but if you allow me to see your material – "

"They're copyrighted."

He smiled. "Then we don't have to worry about anyone stealing your material. Good. Good."

He stood, told me, "You may send your report and bill to me." He winked at me. "You used the exact amount I gave you, I'm sure."

I nodded and he patted Alizée's shoulder and said, "I hope you will allow me the privilege. If you have any songs as good as *How Could You Leave Me*, then multiple checks like these will be commonplace."

He waved to me. "I'll let myself out." He did.

Alizée looked at the checks again, called them out to me without looking up.

"Mercury Productions, $900."

"Camp Records, $492."

"Duchess Records, $1,283."

I let out a whistle. "Over $2,600 dollars. Not bad. Why don't we go to your bank and then we can have lunch."

She sat back and closed her eyes and I watched her chest rise and fall, saw her face shading red and in the back of my mind I heard her mother's broken voice –

How could you leave our love?
How could you leave me?
How could you leave our world,
and the nights we set afire?
Our nights, Babe. Our streets, Babe
Marigny. Frenchmen. Piety and Desire

THE LARGEST MOVIE house in the city, the Saenger Theatre, took up the entire narrow block of Canal Street between Rampart and Basin with Iberville Street behind it. Its huge semicircular marquee with SAENGER atop, listed two movies playing: *The Mating Season* with Gene Tierney and John Lund and *The Lemon Drop Kid* with Bob Hope and Marilyn Maxwell. I'd fallen a little in love with Gene Tierney when I saw *Laura* and now she was mating. *Lord.*

A frizzy haired girl in the ticket booth acknowledged *Alice in Wonderland* was a special advanced showing matinee Saturday and Sunday only. Jeannie skipped ahead of us down the long atrium of a theatre that sat over four thousand people. Alizée wore a light, white short-sleeved sweater over a dark blue poodle skirt, white socks and black-and-white Buster Browns, her long hair back in a pony-tail. Glad I wore a casual shirt, tan, with light-weight black slacks, since she looked like a Bobby-soxer.

Except her face. This wasn't the shy, wet girl who Kirk brought to my building. Her face should be on a movie magazine cover, those dark eyes and full lips. I tried not to stare but saw the make-up was light on her face, but effective, her eyes shadowed in azure, just a hint of rouge on her cheeks. She wore a dark shade of red lipstick that almost matched her auburn hair. Of course the light sweater showed off her bustline, which had been hidden previously.

There was a Mickey Mouse cartoon followed by a Road Runner cartoon, then an installment of a Republic serial *Government Agents vs. Phantom Legion*. We munched popcorn and sipped Cokes as foreign agents hijacked a shipment of Defense Department Material and government agents were called in. There was a Bugs Bunny cartoon, but no classical music, then a few trailers of upcoming movies – one with a leaping Gene Kelly and a pretty good looking Leslie Caron called *An American in Paris*. Another was a gritty-looking cop movie called *Detective Story* starring Kirk Douglas and Eleanor Parker, along with a dumb looking Ronald Reagan getting upstaged by a chimpanzee in *Bedtime for Bonzo*, which Jeannie wanted to see, of course. Kids love idiots.

Had to admit, the art in *Alice* was extraordinary up on the big screen and we're soon with Alice chasing a white rabbit who's late for an important date. Thankfully, the Bobby-soxer next to me kept me from falling asleep. Twice.

"I liked the Cheshire Cat most of all." Jeannie took my hand as we stepped out. "Who did y'all like the most?"

I looked at Alizée who said she liked the Mad Hatter. I said I liked the Dormouse because he kept falling asleep and Alizée took my other hand and squeezed it as we moved along the atrium. Couples filtered in for the early show and I spied a face looking at me and barely kept my eyes from bulging as Helen Bern stepped in front of us. She wore a slimming gray dress with a crimson scarf and black heels, a pearl necklace around her throat. Her left arm was wrapped around the arm of a man with gray-white hair. Taller than me, the man wore a silver suit with a black tie pinned to his starched white shirt by a diamond tie-tack.

"Lucien," Helen said, "I didn't know you had children."

She introduced Sir Evelyn Saint John, the British Counsel, and I introduced my daughter and Miss Alizée Diluviennes, a Hollywood songwriter.

"Movie songwriter?"

"She wrote the song *How Could You Leave Me*, sung by Wanda Murphy in Orson Welles's *Dark Heart*. Lena Horne just released the song with an orchestra backup."

Helen explained to Sir Evelyn how I was a private investigator who helped her once with a matter of thievery. She extended a hand covered in a white glove for me to shake.

"It's so nice seeing you again." Helen smiled at Jeannie, then Alizée. "Your ensemble matches perfectly."

"Thank you."

I got us the hell out of there, slipping on my sunglasses when we got out on Canal Street.

"She was a pretty lady, Daddy."

"For a moment," Alizée said. "I thought it was father-daughter day at the Saenger."

Nice. Right over Jeannie's head but right on target.

I laughed and took their hands to lead them down Canal Street. We passed the big department stores, five-and-ten cent stores, ladies shoe stores while cars parked along the widest main street in America, or so I've been told. Streetcars rattled along the neutral ground and boat whistles echoed from the riverfront.

"After we eat, can we come back here, Daddy?"

I hoped Jeannie meant Woolworths or Kress rather than the big department stores.

"Sure, Sweetie."

Jeannie looked at Alizée. "Can we walk and do *Jabberwocky* at the same time?"

"We have to walk slowly." Alizée took her hand and recited softly, in a spooky voice –

"Twas brillig, and the slithy toves
Did gyre and gimble in the wabe;
All mimsey were the borogoves,
And the mome raths outgrabe.
'Beware the Jabberwock, my son!
The jaws that bite, the claws that catch!"

Only a few people seemed to notice and I realized I never read anything like this in a Sam Spade or a Philip Marlowe novel, a Private Eye walking with a daughter and a pretty girl reciting a nonsense poem. I didn't forget I was a PI, watching for a fat man and olive skinned men in a green car, just in case.

Eventually, we turned down Bourbon Street. Thankfully there were no strip joints in the first block of Bourbon, just newsstands, bars, stores, a few buildings converted into apartment houses. We turned down Iberville to Acme Oyster House just as *Jabberwocky* ended. We had to wait ten minutes for a table while people bustled in and out of the skinny restaurant. The place smelled of cooked seafood, sharp and mouth-watering.

A blond waitress who looked maybe twenty, with a beehive hairstyle, sat us at a corner table. Her uniform had the name 'Alice' on it and Jeannie jumped as she sat down.

"We just saw *Alice in Wonderland*."

The waitress blew a pink bubble, popped her gum and said, "Story of my life." She put three menus in front of us. "I live in freakin' wonderland."

I couldn't stop laughing which got Alizée giggling and Jeannie joining in. I got it under control before Alice returned with three glasses of water and asked Alizée if she liked oysters. She did, so I ordered a full oyster loaf for me and half loaves for them, along with French Fries and three Barq's root beers.

"What you said was funny." I passed the menus back to our waitress.

"Funny but true." She gave me a half smile.

This was my kind of place, noisy, inexpensive, full of working class people and good food.

"You remember the Road Runner cartoon?" I asked Jeannie.

"Yeah?"

"That stuff Wile Coyote uses from Acme – "

"Yeah?"

"This is where it comes from." I pointed to the neon lights in the window. "Acme."

Jeannie looked at Alizée for confirmation and got a shrug.

The Barq's came with glasses of ice and we sipped the extra-sweet root beer with bite because extra caffeine came with Barq's. The oyster loaves came fast and we ate the po-boys of French bread and deep-fried oysters, dipping fries into ketchup, wiping our mouths as we ate.

In the Saenger, when I was drifting to sleep, my mind had wandered back to the foreign gangsters who sounded like rough Frenchmen and thought of a question for Alizée. Wasn't sure I should broach the subject, but I did anyway.

"What does your father look like?"

She stopped chewing, tilted her head to the side.

"Sandy hair, light brown eyes, tall, thin."

"Dark skinned?"

"No. Fair."

I nodded. Took a hit of Barq's.

"He was a clown in a traveling circus."

I caught the root beer with my napkin before I coughed it on my daughter.

"A trapeze clown in a French circus." Alizée was serious. Jeannie was into the story, sitting up and staring. "He fell in love with my mother when the circus came to New Orleans and stayed here."

I took a bite of oyster loaf. She dipped a fry in ketchup, bit it in half.

"What made you ask about my Papa?"

My eyes moved to Jeannie, then back. "We'll talk about it later, OK?"

"You don't want to talk in front of me, right?" Jeannie didn't miss much.

"That's right."

"Why? Is it bad?"

"No. Sometimes adults need to talk about adult things."

"Who's an adult except you?"

I laughed but Alizée hadn't smiled since I brought up her father. I pointed to her, then me. The adults.

"Alizée's not an adult," Jeannie said, digging a fry into the mound of ketchup on her plate and popping it into her mouth.

"Yes, she is."

Jeannie waited to finishing chewing. "Teenagers are not adults. Yet."

"Who said I'm a teenager?" Alizée said.

"You aren't?"

"I'm twenty-five."

Jeannie's mouth dropped open. "You … you … don't look –"

Alizée smiled. "Thank you."

My daughter looked at me for help.

I did my best. "Mistaking a lady's younger than she looks is OK. Telling a lady she looks older than she is, well, don't ever do that."

"Unless you want to make her mad," Alizée said. "I will teach you these things, Jeannie. OK?"

"Yeah."

Alizée looked at me without expression and damn, she was so damn pretty.

A TRAIL OF toilet paper snaked through the living room with Harri at the end of it. On her back, she flailed at the paper, fluttering it, not even noticing us until Jeannie scooped her and she let out a, "Rowl."

The kitten's eyes were even wider than normal.

Alizée pet her head. "You didn't give this kitten catnip, did you?"

Jeannie's eyes became wide and I knew she'd sneaked some of the catnip out of the cupboard.

The three females went into Jeannie's room while I stepped into the kitchen to start up supper. We'd stopped by the French Market for fresh andouille Cajun sausage, a box of ready-made dirty rice, two loaves of French bread and a dozen pralines for dessert.

Jeannie was the first one out with the new yellow dress we bought at D. H. Holmes. She stood in the living room and did a slow turn for me, looking cute as hell. Harri raced out as she headed back into the bedrooms with the kitten wheeling to follow. The next dress looked the same but in dark blue and Harri came rambling out after Jeannie.

"You look very nice, young lady."

She went back in and Alizée stepped out in a white dress with flower prints, red, pink and blue.

"It's a sunshine swing dress," she told me with a roll of her eyes. It had spaghetti straps, fitted to midriff and flared below.

"What about the other dress?" The one from Maison Blanche.

"You're going to have to ask me out to see that one on me." She opened her mouth and smiled, turned and went to change back in her Bobby-sox outfit. The second dress was a black number with spaghetti straps as well but made of a stretchy looking material, a body-hugging mid-calf dress far shorter than most post war dresses.

Yep. This was no teen-ager. Hell, she'd been on her own since her mother died in '44.

Did pretty well with supper. Hard to mess up. All I had to do was warm the dirty rice and fry the andouille. Jeannie said she hadn't made up her mind if she liked andouille – pork sausage, highly seasoned with red pepper, onions and other spices, or boudin – sausage made with rice, pork, chicken and vegetables.

Jeannie spotted the wall clock and hustled into her bedroom with Harri in pursuit and Alizée helped me with the dishes, which we finished just as my doorbell rang. I hit the buzzer, went out on the landing to see Kirk Eckland in uniform wave up at me and start up the stairs.

"Thought I'd check to see if you heard any more from our Alice."

Our Alice. Funny guy.

I let him in and nodded to Alizée standing in between the kitchen area and the living room and wiping her hands with a towel. Eckland froze, looked at me.

"Well, I guess she's OK." He tugged up his utility belt, smiling at Alizée. "This is a nice cozy domestic scene."

Hold Me, Babe

Jeannie hustled in carrying Harri and her Captain Video secret code template, which came in the mail yesterday, along with her decoder ring, which was on her right finger.

"Hi, Mr. Kirk." She hurried to the TV and turned it on.

Eckland was still smirking at me. Didn't he just call this a domestic scene?

I moved past Alizée and she winked at me and I started up a pot of coffee-and-chicory.

"Want some?" I asked Eckland who was checking out Alizée.

"Can't stay." He backed toward the door. "Got a new rookie partner downstairs. Antsy as hell. He might drive off if something breaks on the radio."

I nodded to him and told him I'll walk down with him.

"Dad. Dad. It's coming on in eleven minutes."

"I'll be right back."

Alizée stepped over to Jeannie and asked what's coming on.

"*Captain Video and his Video Rangers.*"

Alizée shook her head and I told her, "You prefer Liberace?"

"No."

Eckland chuckled all the way down the stairs.

"It's not that funny."

"Hell, I thought I was a fast mover but you trumped me with this one."

"Well, I'm not the only one looking for her."

We moved out on the banquette to his black prowl car with the white NOPD star-and-crescent badge painted on the passenger door and a blond haired rookie sitting behind the wheel.

"Not the only one?" Eckland stretched his back.

"A balding fat man, 5'9", 280 pounds, big moustache in a black Cadillac asked the priest over at Saint Alphonsus about Alizée, then two olive skinned men, one about 5'6" with a thick moustache and scar on his left cheek, with a foreign accent, sounding French but looking Portuguese, asked the same priest about her. They were in a green Chevy or Olds."

"Fuck. Did she tell you what that could be about?"

"Not yet."

"I'll keep an eye out and let the boys at the precinct know, since she's right there on Burgundy." Eckland laughed again and slapped my shoulder. "She's not staying here, is she?"

"No."

He turned and told his partner, "This man's getting old, watching Captain Video on TV." He folded his arms, looked back at me. "Wasn't long ago you were trimming a luscious babe on the sofa in your office then later that night humped her daughter up in your apartment. What? Only last year you were having carnal knowledge of that scrumptious Callie chick *and* that Greta Garbo look-a-like from Paris. Simultaneously. What?"

I backed away toward the door.

"The Bobby-soxer has promise," he added.

"Get lost."

The Video Ranger was on screen, slipping a ring on his finger. Jeannie looked back and showed her Dad she had the same ring and the ranger explained this was the 'secret identifying ring'. And I thought it was a decoder ring. According to the teen-aged Video Ranger, this was the most important piece of equipment for all qualified 'video agents'. It must be worn at all times to show you are on the side of Captain Video fighting for law and order.

I sat next to Alizée on the sofa with Jeannie on the floor with Harri, nearer the TV.

"Did you actually send two powerhouse candy bar rappers in to get the ring?"

"What do you think?" I nodded to the TV. "Jeannie has a crush on the teen-aged Video Ranger."

My daughter's head snapped around and she glared at me.

"He is cute," said Alizée. "What's his name?"

Jeannie huffed. "I've been trying to find out. They just call him the Video Ranger."

"I'll bet it's Biff or Chip." I said. "Maybe Scooter."

Jeannie bulged her eyes at me while Alizée tried not to laugh.

Apparently that was a Powerhouse candy bar commercial because we went back to the show and Captain Video, Master of Space and Champion of Justice, along with his trusted sidekick, the Video Ranger, both wearing white football helmets, were in pursuit of two evil schemers who escaped their electronic manacles and were loose aboard the spaceship *Polar Star*.

JEANNIE FINALLY GOT sleepy and took Harri into her bedroom. We turned off the TV and sat at either end of my sofa, Alizée and I each sipping a cold Beck's dark beer.

"Where did you get this?"

"Royal Hayden Wine Cellar on Magazine. Same place I get my friend John's beer. Wells Bombardier."

Beck's was heavy lager and delicious chilled to almost freezing.

"I meant to ask if you'd prefer being called Alice."

She shook her head. "You're the only person calling me Alizée. The sisters at Saint Alphonsus insisted I be called Alice since there was a Saint Alice."

"St. Alice Through the Looking-glass or Wonderland?" I grinned.

"No, Saint Alice the Jumper, patron saint of kangaroos and bullfrogs."

We both laughed. Obviously, we'd both survived Catholic education by nuns. I've been telling people for years I was named after Saint Lucien the Smoocher, patron saint of the black eye.

She had her shoes and socks off, her feet tucked under her skirt as she leaned against the end of the sofa. I was at the other end with my shoes off as well, a nice cool breeze flowing through the transoms.

"You said you wrote twenty-six other songs. All blues?"

"Some rhythm and blues, like Fats Domino's songs. Rockin' blues, even some folk ballads. I have a guitar and I can use the piano downstairs at the boarding house when everyone's awake or away."

"Any recorded besides *How Could You Leave Me?*"

She shook her head, took another hit of Beck's. Her eyes were dark agates in the dim light, her face smooth and the lines of her cheeks taut, her full lips dark red.

"I write pretty much all the time. I hear tunes in my brain and match words to them."

We each took another swig of beer.

"I know a writer," I said.

"Who?"

"Tennessee Williams."

She took a sip. "I thought we were being serious."

"I am. I met Thomas some years ago. Helped him out of a jam when he lived on Saint Peter Street." Where he wrote "*Streetcar.*"

She sat up. "*A Streetcar Named Desire.*"

"That would be the one."

She leaned toward me. "I would *love* to meet him."

"He's in New York at the moment, left me a copy of his latest play *The Rose Tattoo*. It's down in my office. When he comes back in town he usually calls and I'll make sure you meet."

She kept staring into my eyes, a slight smile on those lips.

"I'm serious," I said. "He appreciates a pretty girl."

"I heard he was – "

"Tennessee Williams understands women better than any man I'll ever know."

We finished our beers at the same time just as Harri came bounding into the room and headed straight for us. No. She spotted my shoes and attacked a shoestring. Alizée got on her hands and knees on the sofa and moved to me in a feline crawl, shoulders rolling. She licked her lips and drew close and I put a hand on her cheek and brought my lips to hers.

The soft kiss sent a wave through my body, a kiss that went on for almost a minute, maybe more, not getting any hotter but not needing to. She pulled back, sat next to me, still looking at me. She let out a long breath.

"Wow."

"You tellin' me?"

She closed her eyes and I stared at her face in profile, that small, upturned nose, the full lips and small chin.

"What perfume do you wear?" I'd been smelling it, but now, up close, it seemed more intense.

"Caliari. It's Italian. You like it?"

"Oh, yes." Hell, there wasn't anything I didn't like about this girl.

"I'm going to have to watch myself with you, Mister." Her eyes were still closed. "You're dangerous."

"Yeah?"

"Just give me a little time, OK?"

Time? She was ahead of me again.

"Don't give up on me, Lucien."

"Why would I do that?"

"Everyone else has." She smiled. "I'm not being melodramatic. It's just happened that way. Even my Papa gave up on me." Her eyes opened and she looked at me. "Which reminds me. What made you ask about my Papa?"

The way my heart stammered, it was better we talked business.

"Some other men are looking for you." I told her about the fat man, then about the men who could be French. "So I had to know if one was your father."

Her brow furrowed. "Looking for me?"

I nodded and felt a sharp pain on the back of my neck. Harri scrambled to the top of my head and hung on. It took some careful caressing of the kitten to get her off without any damage beyond a few pulled hairs. I held her up and she swatted at me. I laid her on her back and ticked her belly and she flailed. I stoked her and she stopped wiggling and began purring.

"When did your father leave y'all?"

"April, 1938. I was twelve." She closed her eyes again. "What if these men show up where I work, or live?"

"Call the police right away and call me." I put Harri up on her feet and petted her head and she purred again.

"I'll be looking for them, of course."

"You're going to tear the mirrors off their cars?" She smiled sadly at me.

"Probably worse."

"Can you really be mean?" She shook her head. "Your eyes are too soft for you to be mean."

I leaned over and kissed her again, longer, more passionately. Harri separated us, wiggling between us and crying. Alizée laughed and Harri scrambled back into the bedrooms, for Jeannie most likely. I pulled Alizée across my body and we kissed and kept kissing. No tongues. Not yet. We kept ourselves under control and the necking was very nice.

I left a note for Jeannie, telling her I was bringing Alizée home and to call Uncle John if she needed anything. She knew how to call the police in case it was bad, but I made sure all the balcony doors were locked and the apartment locked, as well as the downstairs doors. The night shift cat was on the hood of a car parked behind mine. He watched me check under my hood.

Alizée sat close to me.

"I thought of taking Jeannie to the zoo tomorrow. Wanna come along?"

"I'll be writing in the morning. What time are you going?"

"After lunch."

"Yes, I'd like to come along." She bumped me with her shoulder and smiled.

"You have another poodle-skirt?"

"Why?"

"I like going out with teen-agers."

She poked my shoulder. "She has her eyes on you, that Miss-Elegant-I'm-With-Sir-What's His Name."

"She's too old for me."

Found a parking spot, incredibly, and I walked her to her door where we kissed goodnight. She held on to my shirt as we pulled apart.

"You're going to find those men looking for me?"
"I'll lay a trap for them."
"Why are they looking for me?"
"I'll find out."
She narrowed that right eye again.
"Have you ever hurt anyone badly?"
I nodded slowly. "Only Nazis and criminals."

I WASN'T SURPRISED when Helen called Monday.
"Join me for lunch? Holmes Café. Noon?"
"Sure."
I wasn't sure but what the hell.

I went back to my morning paper. The Rosenbergs were sentenced to death. *No shit.* The judge described their crime as 'worse than murder'. He had a point but even an enlisted man like me knew military advances like the Atom Bomb had limited exclusivity. If our scientists could figure it out, someone else on earth could as well. It was only a matter of time. Then again, the Rosenbergs gave the commies a short cut.

I switched to an article about NOPD. A visiting AP reporter named Kohn painted an ugly picture of my former department. Graft, vice, refusing to stop prostitution and gambling. He didn't mention the nearly non-existent murder rate and the fact NOPD concentrated on robbery and burglary cases. Vice and New Orleans went together like beans and rice.

Mr. Kohn seemed to recognize this, to his credit. He was from Chicago, said people up there were usually on one side of the fence or the other – criminal or law-abiding citizen.

Crooked politician or honest politician. In New Orleans there was no fence.

I DROVE PAST Alizée's boarding house on Burgundy Street and where she worked over on Julia Street. No Cadillac or green Chevy or Olds, so I tooled back to Canal Street, found a meter a block from D. H. Holmes Department Store, a huge store with picture windows of manikins with the latest fashions facing Canal. When I was shopping with the girls and reading the fashion section of the newspaper, I saw dresses and skirts just keep getting longer. During the war, with the shortage of material, women were forced to wear shorter skirts, not that I heard any complaint. This new conservative look was boring.

Helen Bern sat in the airy restaurant at the rear of the store, at a side table next to the windows looking out Dauphine Street. Smelling of roses, rather than food, ceiling fans cooling the lunch crowd, women mostly, dressed up to the nines. The men were either old or around twenty, twenty-one, smug looking gigolos. I was the only man around thirty.

Helen wore a Dior number, fitted but long, beige with a white swatch in front that looked like a bib from a distance. She lifted a martini glass as I sat across from her. The waiter was there right away, a middle-aged man who wore too much Old Spice after shave.

"The lady has ordered, sir."

I handed him the menu lying next to my plate and ordered a chicken salad sandwich on a croissant which came with extra thin French fries.

"To drink?"

"Iced tea." Which came sweetened here in New Orleans.

Helen waited until we were alone and smiled. "The songwriter. She a girlfriend or a babysitter?"

"Is that what you want to talk about?"

My tea arrived and Helen waited for the waiter to step away.

"What did you think we would talk about?"

She was a good looking woman, most definitely one of the chic dames I considered my M.O. Only there was something predatory about her. I almost laughed at my train of thought. The last few women in my life were all predators – Callie, the avaricious beauty who left love for money, Rochette, who helped a man kill himself, and the rapacious Madelyn Croix who devoured men like a hawk feasting on field mice.

"Lucien, you still there?"

"Yes. Um, I thought you might need help with another piece of purloined jewelry."

Our croissants arrived. No surprise we'd ordered the same thing. The Holmes Café was known for its chilled chicken salad with poppy seed dressing.

She waited for the waiter to leave to give me a sly smile and said, wide-eyed, "I sent my driver home with my shopping, so can you take me home when we're finished?"

Jesus. I told her yes, I could.

I didn't know about this little sex game she was playing. It was nice clearing out the pipes with her the other day. Having a daughter had put a kink in my sex life, so a little emotionless piece on the side was fine. But this wasn't that at all. Was it?

She confirmed it when she went back to her initial inquiry.

"How old is the Bobby-soxer?"

LEAVING A MIFFED Helen Bern at her mansion without going in for a little personal attention, I headed to the

Irish Channel, since I was uptown. I'm not used to telling a willing woman no, but if women could say no, why couldn't men, even if it caught in my throat. She shouldn't have called Alizée 'the Bobby-soxer'.

Father Callan was out front again.

"If you don't watch them carefully, all your parishioners will just run amok won't they?"

"What?" Mickey Rooney put his fists on his hips. "That supposed to be funny?"

So far I had everyone mad at me today. I just grinned at the little sucker.

"I called you three times since eleven. You do not have an answering service."

He was right. Been meaning to link up with one.

"What's up, Father?"

"The fat man came back. He still won't leave his name and he'd taken the license plate off his Cadillac."

"Anything else you notice?"

"He had a cigar this time."

"What did he ask, exactly?"

"He was looking for the daughter of Wanda Murphy."

"Did he mention the daughter's name?"

"No. He asked me her name."

"Don't give anyone her name." I resisted poking him in the chest. "Not anyone."

I looked around. Not a soul out on Constance Street. No, an old woman was crossing the street a little ways off.

"You have a gun, Father?"

"No."

"Get one. Next time he comes, shoot out his radiator. That'll keep him here."

I started away, stopped, thanked him for calling.

"The foreigners haven't been back, have they?"

"No." The priest's face lit up. "Oh, the fat man. He said he was a detective."

"Police?"

He opened his arms.

"Show you a badge?"

"No."

Bald, fat man with a moustache. Cigar. Detective. No badge.

Oh, no.

I'D CHECKED ON Alizée at work earlier and called her after I got home. I didn't mention the fat man.

"Mrs. Woodruff fixed her special chicken fricassee. She'll call me down soon and if we're late we don't get dessert. Have you ever had Mississippi Mud?"

"Not on purpose."

"It's a wonder with pecans and cream cheese, milk chocolate pudding, vanilla pudding, whipped cream and covered with shavings from a dark chocolate bar."

I told her Kaye was teaching Jeannie how to cook red beans and stuffed mirlitons for supper tonight and asked if she had plans for supper the next night.

"Not really."

"Good. Have you ever had cochon de lait ravioli?"

"What?"

I leaned back on my sofa and explained how my friend Dino Nuzzolillo at the Central Grocery invented stuffing ravioli with Cajun cochon de lait – suckling pig, well seasoned and roasted for six hours, ground up and stuffed into ravioli to be served with garlic marinara sauce.

"I have to get it to go, take it home because there are no tables at the grocery."

"I've been there but never had cochon de lait ravioli."

Hold Me, Babe

"Then you are in for a culinary delight."

There was a noise behind her and Alizée said it was supper time.

"Can I call you back later?"

"Seven o'clock would be perfect," I said. "Captain Video will be just starting."

She laughed and said, "Oh. How's Jeannie's hand?"

"Fine. She learned monkeys aren't kittens."

We hung up and I waited with Harri for Jeannie and Kaye to call that supper's ready. The kitten sandwiched herself between me and the back of the sofa and purred loudly as I pet her little head and thought about Jeannie standing outside the monkey cage at the zoo on Sunday, her hand up on the fence railing. I had turned away for three snowballs and saw it from a distance, too far away to warn her the spider monkey moving to the cage bars had a yardstick in its hand. It reached the yardstick out and Jeannie just watched until the damn primate slapped her hand with the yardstick.

The zookeeper had no clue who gave the monkey a yardstick, except to say, "They are pretty good thieves."

THE WORST PRIVATE detective in New Orleans, maybe in America, had an office in the Carondelet Building but I wasn't about to be kept cooling my heels in a waiting room. The fat fuck lived in Faubourg Marigny, just below the French Quarter on Touro Street.

At seven a.m., I knocked on his door, hard. It was a shotgun house painted light gray. I knocked again and kept knocking until I heard his voice call out, "Who's there?"

"Open up, Ian. I brought donuts."

The door opened and a man standing 5'9", weighing two-ninety, nearly completely bald now, blinked his beady eyes at me. He wore an undershirt and red and white striped boxer underwear.

"I hear you're looking for Wanda Murphy's daughter."

He looked at my hands.

"I thought you said 'donuts'."

"You wanna talk out here or you're gonna invite me in?"

His rotundity nodded, backed away and left the door open. I stepped into a dark living room that smelled of furniture polish. Ian Allacula waved to one of the two sofas and said he'd be right back and went into the next room, closing the door. As my eyes adjusted to the room, I saw it was surprisingly clean. I sat on a tan sofa and waited.

Owner and operator of AA Detective Agency, Allacula was a sleezeball. I saw him get a man killed by sloppy investigation. He told a man the man's wife was having an affair with a co-worker who the man shot to death only the dead co-worker was more interested in men than women and was providing a sympathetic shoulder to a 'girlfriend'.

The fat man came out in a robe, sat across from me in a large armchair.

"OK, Lucy, what you got for me?"

Lucy?

"I have the daughter. Why are you looking for her?"

"Client hired me."

I knew better than ask who, so I asked, "What for?"

He smiled and looked like a bullfrog. "Why don't we cut a deal. I'll split my fee. All I want is to locate the daughter. Deliver a message."

"You don't even know her name."

"It's something Murphy. If you found her, I will."

"OK, give me the message and we'll split the fee."

He shook his head. "It's a private message from a father to his daughter."

Did the idiot just tell me who his client is?
I hoped my face didn't give it away. *Her father? Wasn't the fool in France?*

"OK. You're in touch with the father and I'm in touch with the daughter." The lazy bastard will take the easy way out if I offered it. "I'll ask if she wants a sit-down and call you. If she wants no part of her father, you won't hear from me and you won't find her."

I stood as a large lizard came in into the living room from in back.

"No need to be afraid. Billy is an iguana. They don't bite."

I left the bullfrog and his lizard, went straight to Morning Call Coffee Stand for a couple cups of strong coffee-and-chicory café au lait and the morning *Eagle*. The narrow coffeehouse sat in a triangular building where Decatur Street and North Peters merged, Dumaine Street behind with the wharves and Mississippi River on the other side of North Peters, so we were entertained by ship's whistles as I sat at the long marble counter beneath an archway of lights.

Normally I pass on the beignets but the smell of sugar drew me and I had an order of three, sprinkling powdered sugar from a tin shaker on the deep-fried donuts-without-holes that were so hot, I could almost taste hot oil still on them. The coffee was strong enough to keep a spoon standing straight up. Almost.

According to the front page, his Majesty, General of the Army Douglas MacArthur was about to ignite World War III while President Truman was reminding everyone the president was actually the commander-in-chief. We were being tested about civilian control of the military. Didn't help with MacArthur complaining about 'temporary occupants of the White House'.

I turned to the sports section and read more about Mickey Mantle. Yankees manager Stengel said when he watched Mantle run wind-sprints and had Mickey run again, against the entire team. Stengel declared the boy was faster than Ty Cobb, which was something for sure. The article went on about Mantle maybe being the most powerful switch-hitter – ever. Most couldn't hit the long ball consistently, but not Mantle. He was a natural homerun hitter from both sides of the plate. In one exhibition game, Mantle blasted five homers and was batting over .400 this spring training season.

THE DAY SHIFT tomcat, the orange tabby, sat atop the Cabrini park fence when I parked the Ford and Alizée climbed out with me. She wore a white blouse with the collar turned up and tight dungarees that caressed her body nicely, her long hair hanging straight around that pretty face, red lipstick drawing my eyes to her full lips.

"They aren't called dungarees anymore," she'd told me when I complemented her. "They're blue jeans."

The ravioli, covered in marinara sauce, was incredible and I was glad I waited until after we ate to tell Alizée about the fat man so she could enjoy supper. After putting Jeannie and Harri to bed, I settled with Alizée on my sofa, close to her, facing her.

"The fat man is a private detective. Not a very good one. He thinks your last name is Murphy."

"The fat man asking Father Callan about me?"

I nodded, watched her eyes and said, "He says he has a private message for you from your father."

She rocked back, blinked twice and closed her eyes, her chest rising as she took in a deep breath.

"Is my Papa here?"

"I don't know.'

She opened her eyes and they were damp. She closed them again.

"I don't know what I should do, Lucien."

"There's no rush."

"Do you think the fat man will find me if I don't want to —"

"Not likely. Ian Allacula, that's his name, is lazy and when he adds two and two, he usually comes up with three."

"You found me."

"I'm a lot sharper."

"Does he have friends like Kirk Eckland?"

"Nope. NOPD hates Ian Allacula. And I would have found you without Kirk."

"Yes?"

"I was setting up a surveillance of Varenne Maritime Law. I'd have spotted you. He'll never trace you there." No way I could see his rotundity following leads to Cypress Grove Cemetery.

She wiped her eyes. "What about the other men looking for me?"

"They could be French. Could be connected with your father too."

I had hopes for a little smooching because I'm half French and half Spanish with enough hormones that have given me uncontrolled erections since I was fourteen. Don't judge me. I could have waited until after we cuddled for an hour or two before telling her.

"I need to think this out."

We sat side-by-side and she closed her eyes again. I felt her arm against mine and settled back, closed my eyes. It was warm in the apartment even with the transoms open and the ceiling fans moving and my eye-lids grew heavy.

I didn't feel her move until her lips touched mine and my eye-lids snapped open. Her eyes were closed and we kissed and kissed again and French kissed until we were both panting and she pulled back. My hand was on her ass, rubbing it and she looked back at it.

"It's got a mind of its own," I told her.

"It's getting late, Babe. I go to work early." She stood and raised her hands behind her head, arched her back, those breasts right in front of my face. She smiled at me, said we have to find a better place to neck.

"I keep thinking Jeannie's gonna come out, catching you copping a feel."

"I haven't copped a feel, yet."

"You grabbed my butt."

She scooped her purse, headed for the door. "I was thinking, what's stopping you?" She stuck out her tongue and I hurried after her. When we got downstairs, I pointed to my office door, told her about the oversized davenport sofa, special made by the Chipping Bubbly Company of Boston, Massachusetts.

"I've slept down there many times waiting for clients to come in the middle of the night."

"Come? For some personal attention?"

"No," I lied. "Because they were either scared or mental cases."

"Yeah." She flipped her hair aside as we stepped out. "Right."

SO THE SULLIVAN Slushy case was over. That's what Ernest Brienne thought. I didn't.

The sun seemed extra bright, billowy clouds rose to the stratosphere like huge cotton balls and I found a parking spot right on Saint Charles Avenue.

Hold Me, Babe

I leaned on the buzzer outside the wrought iron gate of the Academie de Jeanne d'Arc. A streetcar rattled behind me and an automobile's brakes squealed. I turned to see a car had stopped short on the neutral ground, the driver leaning on his horn now. Idiot didn't know the streetcar always has the right of way. I pushed the buzzer again and waited.

It took four more pushes before a female voice, sounding tinny on the intercom, asked, "What is it?"

"I have an appointment with Mother Superior. My name's Caye."

Three streetcars and eleven minutes later, an Arcasian nun in black habit and huge white, seagull winged head-dress unlocked the gate, told me to wait until she relocked as if I would run amok. She was young, maybe twenty, pretty but not overly so and did not meet my eyes as she led me through a beautiful garden of white and red rose bushes, pink azaleas in bloom and red camellias and into the smaller of the two buildings and through an immaculately clean hall.

We went through double doors to an office area with four desks, all unoccupied.

"Lunch time," the sister explained. "Staff helps at the cafeteria."

The door was marked 'Mother Superior-Principal' and the nun behind the small desk looked more like Mr. Bogardus from *The Bells of Saint Mary's* than Ingrid Bergman.

She did not seem to remember I'd called that morning until I reminded her I was the man who said, "Yes, ma'am." And she'd corrected me – it was "Yes, sister."

"Sit down." She pointed to a stiff back chair in front of her desk. "I am Sister Mary Constance and I do not have a lot of time for a *private* detective."

So I got right to it.

"Sullivan Slushy."

I watched those little eyes grow narrower.

"Do you happen to have a list of the girls who accused him of, well, girls he tomcatted around?"

She jumped in her chair like I'd pinched her butt.

"That is none of your business."

"I know that. But I'm more discreet than a Grand Jury Subpoena. You really want to testify in front of a dozen nosy grand jurors?"

She snatched up the phone, looked at the dial, hung up and sat up straighter.

"You do know the confidentiality of the confessional applies to priests only, sister."

"I will not discuss Mr. Slushy until I am forced to."

I knew that, knew she wouldn't tell me anything. I was about to ask her how many girls he'd impregnated but didn't want a yardstick batting me over the head.

"You may go now." Her gaze moved to the two yardsticks I had spotted when I came in.

"You didn't lose one of those at the zoo, huh sister?" I stood and thanked her for her time.

"You're not welcome." She waved an index finger at me. "I intend to call Brother Andrew at Holy Cross and tell him I did not appreciate this one bit."

"It's not his fault I'm a pain in the butt, sister."

"He asked me to talk with you, didn't he?"

I knew this was a long shot but sometimes you take them. I was pretty sure it was more than a couple girls and I was right. How do I find out who? I'd have to figure that out.

The young nun stood outside the door and turned to lead me back out. Something caught my eye as I passed between the desks, something that drew goose bumps on my arms. A name plate on a desk that read 'Mrs. Haverton'.

Haverton? Could this be related to the man who investigated the Sullivan Slushy murder? The drunk detective who drove his car into an oak tree on Carrollton Avenue at sixty miles an hour?

I waited until we were outside.

"I remember when Mrs. Haverton's husband was killed," I said. "Real shame."

"I was new then."

She must have been a teenaged nun.

"She's been here a while hasn't she?"

"Long time, I understand."

The strong scent of roses made me feel like I was in a funeral parlor. I spied a green lizard scamper across the brick walkway.

"You know, I always wondered about the high tuition here."

"What about it?" The sister did not seem in a hurry. Maybe she liked talking to a tall, darkly handsome stranger or maybe she didn't want to go into that cafeteria. The girls couldn't be as rowdy as we were at Holy Cross.

"I figure you only get the daughters of the filthy rich in here."

"Oh, no. We award scholarships to families of lesser means so we do not only educate the daughters of the wealthy. I am on the scholarship committee."

"I didn't catch your name."

She smiled. "I didn't throw it. I am Sister Mary Claudette." She extended a small hand and we shook and she finally looked me in the eye.

"What about your staff?" I said.

"What about it?"

"Do they get a tuition discount for their children?"

She hesitated but only for a moment.

"They get a tuition waiver."

I waited until she was unlocking the gate for my final question.

"Did Mrs. Haverton's daughter manage to get into college?"

"Yes. Dartmouth."

I thanked her and took out a five dollar bill, put it in her hand.

"What's this?"

"A tip."

Her jaw actually dropped. "Sisters do not accept gratuities."

"Thanks, sister." And I went through the gate and did not look back.

My original plan was to shake up mother superior and see if anyone came around to tell me to keep out of it. I had a right to feel clever now. I didn't even know the Havertons had a daughter until now. So my mission changed. It was now – find Mrs. Haverton.

THE HEADLINE READ: Truman fires MacArthur. It came to a head, the general unable to give his support to the president's foreign policy. The topper came when MacArthur told the press the president needed to concentrate on Asia, instead of rebuilding Europe. Use Generalissimo Chang Kai-shek's troops in Formosa to open a second front in China.

There were two accompanying pictures, one of MacArthur talking with his successor Lieutenant General Matthew Ridgway, both in heavy jackets with fur collars. The other picture was General Eisenhower with a surprised look on his face. The caption below that photo said this was Eisenhower's genuine reaction to MacArthur's firing. The president was blunt. Vigorous debate on national policies is acceptable, but military commanders must follow presidential policies and directives.

I remembered Ridgway as the 82nd Airborne commander in Sicily and Normandy, all the way to the Battle of the Bulge. From what I've read, Ridgway was already turning the Korean War around. We'll see if he can finish it without us slipping into WWIII.

The rain rolled in around ten a.m. and stayed hard for an hour before tapering off to a drizzle for another few hours. I caught up on my paperwork, typing up my notes on my two latest cases, then remembered I was supposed to hire an answering service.

I called Annie Fordow right away, started by thanking her for the info on the Briennes.

"Glad it helped. Come up with anything I could use?"

"Not really." *As if I'd get a newspaper involved.*

"So what do you need now?"

I tried laughing, but she didn't sound amused.

"I figured you'd know a good answering service, dependable and not expensive."

She paused a few seconds. "Funny you should ask. My cousin just started one and could use the business."

"Good, what's the number?"

"I don't know."

"What?"

"She's a cutie pie, Lucien, and not that experienced."

That's right. I'm a lothario.

"This is business, Annie."

She gave me the number and I had to admit the soft voice that answered the phone at Your Answer Answering Service sounded a little sexy, a deep, throaty voice.

"I need an answering service."

"Then you called the right place. I'm Bobbie, with an 'ie', what's your name, sir?"

I gave her my name and she let out what sounded like a cough or a hiccup.

"Is this *The* Lucien Caye?"

"No, it's the other one." *What the hell?*

"The Private Eye, I mean."

"Yes. You caught me."

"I read about you in the papers."

Lord.

"There should be a headline atop every newspaper page that reads – FICTION."

She laughed and we got down to business and nine minutes later I had an answering service.

THE BOARDING HOUSE mother, Mrs. Woodruff, let me into the living room, said Alice would be down in a minute. A big woman, at least 5'10" and thick, wore a white apron over a flower-pattern dress and black shoes that looked like short rubber boots. Her gray hair was in a bun around her large head.

"My husband was killed at Chateau-Thierry, July 18, 1918. Were you in the second war?"

"Yes, ma'am."

"What? Soldier, sailor or marine?"

"Army."

The room smelled of perfume. Maybe it was Mrs. Woodruff.

"Where'd you fight?"

"North Africa. Sicily. Italy."

"Kill a lot Germans?"

"Not enough. There are still some left."

Her broad face grinned at me like a Jack-o-lantern.

Alizée stepped in wearing a tan polka-dot dress with a self-tie sash, matching knotted bows atop each shoulder strap and pumps. Her hair hung straight down and, while neatly combed, looked limp and made her look younger than ever.

"Do you like my hair like this?" She said as she sat next to me in my car. "Where's Jeannie tonight?"

"She thinks she's babysitting little Donna while Kaye's making supper, but Charley, that's Kaye's husband, is keeping an eye on the girls. You haven't met Charley. He's a helluva mechanic and I always like your hair."

She rolled her eyes. I knew what she meant of course. Her perfume smelled stronger and unlike many other perfumes, did not overwhelm. I told her I liked her hair like that.

"I don't," she said. "I was trying a new rinse that supposed to control the flyaway look."

"I like the flyaway look," I admitted.

"I think I do too. I'll give the rinse to Mrs. Woodruff. Her hair looks like a Brillo pad."

She pressed her arm and leg against me, asked if we couldn't go to someplace quiet.

"No big place, OK?"

"I was thinking of finding a hot dog vendor on the street."

"OK."

"That was a joke."

I took her to Angelia's Pizzeria on Saint Claude. We sat at the end of one of the long tables, near the ovens and it was hot but not unpleasant. There were only two other couples in the small place and I ordered a pitcher of beer as we waited for our pizza.

The jukebox switched from Miles Davis's *Dig* to *Cold Cold Heart* by Tony Bennett.

"Bennett's good but Hank Williams knows how to sing his songs," she said.

We sipped cold beer, one cook trying to sing along with Tony Bennett, the other arguing with the girl behind the cash register, a youngster in a tight blue sweater.

Alizée focused those dark brown eyes at me. "I think I want to see the message from my Papa, but I don't want to meet that fat man."

The cook called out our pizza was ready and I went and got it – sausage, bacon and extra cheese. Hot and spicy and we started in on it.

"Do you think the fat man will give the message to you for me?"

"I thought of that. If you write a note to your father and seal it. Write it so he knows it's from you. Tell him he can contact you through me. We'll include my address and phone number."

Fats Domino's *Don't You Lie to Me* came on.

"How are your new songs coming along?"

She smiled sadly. "They're coming along."

I almost asked if she'd let me hear some of her songs, but didn't want to put pressure on Alizée the writer. There was something about Miss Diluviennes that was almost fragile. At least, that's what I felt about her sitting there with her straight hair and eating pizza with me.

Hank Williams entertained us with *Hey Good Lookin'*. She was right, of course. The man knew how to sing his songs.

IT WAS HER choice when we got to my building. As I locked the building door she did not even look at my office door and the inviting, oversized Chipping Bubbly inside. I followed her upstairs and we both went down the hall to

Kaye's place and I introduced Alizée to Charley Rudabaugh before we went back to my place to watch another insufferable episode of *Captain Video and his Video Rangers* with Jeannie.

Alizée wasn't there. She sat next to me on the sofa while Harri played with my fingers, but Alizée's mind was far away. I took her hand and she squeezed mine, leaned her head against my shoulder and closed her eyes. Harri slipped between us and started purring.

Jeannie stared at the TV, leaning forward as the Video Ranger got into a fist fight with a man wearing a gas mask, football shoulder pads under a glimmering space suit and a short helmet with a propeller atop.

Later, I tucked my daughter into bed, gave her a goodnight kiss, kissed Harri on the head and made sure the night light was on and the balcony doors locked before going back into the living room to wake Alizée.

She sat up, stretched, asked what she'd missed.

"The Video Ranger beat up the spaceman wearing the gas mask and Captain Video found a naked woman swimming in a one of the canals of Mars. A redhead."

"You saw this on a black and white TV screen?"

"I think I fell asleep too."

I brought a Wells Bombardier across the hall, passed it to John, asked him to listen for Jeannie.

"I'll leave my door open, old chap. 'Til you return."

He bowed slightly to Alizée and raised his beer to her as we stepped away.

On our way downstairs she whispered, "He always has a twinkle in his eye."

"He's a lothario."

"No."

"Oh, yes. The man is smooth with the ladies."

She stopped next to my office door. "Do you have stationery and an envelope in there?"

"Sure."

We went in and I pulled a stationery box and matching envelopes, both plain white without any address, but nicer paper than usual typewriter pulp stock. She spotted one of my Parker t-ball jotter ball point pens in the center drawer as she sat behind my desk, clicked it and wrote on a sheet of paper.

It took her three tries to get it the way she wanted it, asking my exact address. I was on the far side of the desk and she slid the note to me, asked what I thought.

It read – 'Papa, if you have a message for me or want to talk to me, contact private investigator Lucien Caye. He will arrange it'. She signed it 'Allie' and put my address and office phone number and I was immediately glad I had an answering service now.

"He will know it's from me. He's the only person in the world who ever called me 'Allie'."

She folded the note, sealed it in an envelope and wrote 'Papa' on the outside. Left it there for me to deliver to the fat man. On our way out, she pointed to the Chipping Bubbly.

"Looks comfy."

"It's always open."

THE CRAPPY DETECTIVE Ian Allacula shrugged when I handed him Alizée's envelope as he came out of his shotgun house the next morning.

"OK," he said, his bullfrog smile widening on his face. "I'll deliver it."

No shit. I was sure he'd collect his fee first. The man never passed up easy money.

"Care to buy me breakfast, Lucy?"

Who was it that said – 'An idiot is an idiot is an idiot'? Shakespeare? Maybe Groucho Marx.

I just walked off. You can't argue with stupid.

IT WASN'T HARD to find Judy Haverton. She still lived in the house she and her husband bought back in 1935. On Audubon Street. Around the corner and two blocks over from the old Slushy house on Walnut Street. The hard part would be getting her to talk.

I set up at two-thirty, figuring she'd be coming home from school about then. I kept thinking of what I should say to get her to talk. Ten minutes after three, she pulled into the driveway in a gray Ford, same year and model as my car, which I pulled up in front of her house as she walked around to the front door. I smiled at her and called out her name. She stopped, switched her purse from right arm to left. I stopped twenty feet from her, introduced myself, asked if I could speak with her.

She was a small woman, a couple inches above five feet, thin, with graying brown hair and tired blue eyes. No doubt she was a beauty twenty, maybe thirty years ago. She wore a green dress with a brown belt and sensible heels.

"I heard about you visiting the Academy."

I nodded.

"I checked on you. Did you work with my husband?"

"No, ma'am. He was already a detective when I was a patrolman. I never went any higher than that, never worked with him at all."

"Well, I have company coming for supper so you can ask your questions while I cook."

The one-story brick house was stuffy, smelled of cigarette smoke. The ash trays were empty, however and Judy pointed to the kitchen while she went into the back of the house. I stopped in the small dining room, took in the two glass cupboards, one filled with pistols, the other with brass knuckles, switchblades, blackjacks and slapsticks.

She stepped back in. "Alvin was a collector. It's all going to auction next month. I found a dealer in Dallas to handle it for me."

She went into the kitchen and I followed as she put on an apron, reached into the refrigerator and pulled out a plate of sausages. Looked like plain ole pork sausages and she put them in a skillet, but didn't turn on the burner. I watched her fill a stock pot with water, put it on a lit burner before she moved to the table with a bowl of red potatoes to peel and cut.

"You have another knife?"

"You know how to fix potatoes?"

"I was in the army. I'm sure you heard of KP."

A minute later I sat across from her peeling and slicing potatoes into cubes for boiling. I waited for her to look at me again before I said the name, "Sullivan Slushy."

She kept her face from reacting but her eyes sharpened and she did have a knife in her hand.

"Did your daughter tell you about him or did you find out another way?"

She took in a deep breath, her shoulders sinking. She went back to dicing potatoes.

"You know what she told us? Immaculate Conception. She had no idea how she became pregnant because she was still a virgin."

"How long did she stick to that story?"

"Didn't last one night. She wouldn't tell us who the father was. But I figured who it was."

"Alvin blow up over it?"

"It was so odd. He changed overnight. Alvin became the supportive, loving father he never was before. He said helping our girl and our grandchild was the most important thing we could do."

She wouldn't look at me as she sliced potatoes.

Like I'm supposed to believe this.

"That .32 caliber Harlow in the gun cabinet."

The blue eyes locked on to mine now.

"I'm taking it with me. I think the bullet that killed Sullivan came out of that gun."

She sat frozen, staring hard at me now. When she spoke, her voice was deep, even, strong. "I did not give you permission to search my house."

"I'm not a cop. I don't need a search warrant. When I leave, you can call the police and tell them I stole the pistol. When you do, there's no way to keep the results of the firearms exam quiet because the gun will be evidence of my theft. Your only shot at keeping this quiet is to let me handle it."

I finished a potato, put it into the bowl, put the knife next to it, wiped my hands on the dishrag she'd provided and stood up. Her eyes grew wet and she took in another deep breath.

"Alvin left us one thing. His pension. Don't take it from us."

The cabinet was unlocked and I checked and the Harlow was not loaded. I slipped it into my pocket and left.

A dark blue Chevy pulled into the drive behind Judy's Ford and a young, pretty woman with light brown hair stepped out, reached back in for a small boy. She watched me leave and I heard Judy's voice echo in my brain, "His pension. Don't take it from us."

WE HAD A date Saturday night and I paid Kaye to watch Jeannie, although she didn't want the money. I told her if I didn't get Jeannie back in the same condition I left her, I wanted my money back. Donna cinched the deal, running over to hug Jeannie.

I waited in the living room of Alizée's boarding house. The room still smelled like perfume although the only occupant was an old gentleman with pale white skin and jet black hair, deep wrinkles that looked painful when his face changed from surprise – that I stepped into the room – to anger when Mrs. Woodruff said I was a detective before she left to announce me to my date.

"I don't like cops," he said, tugging on his left ear and I noticed his ears were elongated. Really damn long.

"I'm not that kind of detective."

"What kind are you?" His long nose crinkled and I waited for the crevices next to it to splinter and spray blood across the room.

"I'm a private investigator."

"Like Sherlock Holmes, Dupin, Poirot? Don't tell me you're like Mike Hammer. He's an ass."

"He treats Velda so badly," I said.

"Exactly." The man almost rose from the thick armchair. His lips twitched and for a moment he looked a little like a fish.

"I keep telling her to leave him, come work for me. I need a good secretary."

The man grimaced. "Will she come to New Orleans? She may dislike the heat."

"It isn't the heat. It's the stupidity."

Alizée stepped into the doorway.

"Yes, yes," he said. "The humidity."

Alizée stood there and I had to blink twice as I slowly stood.

Her hair, fluffed out in auburn waves, drew my eyes to her dark chocolate eyes, black orbs looking at me, a small smile on lips painted dark crimson. She wore a slim, dark blue dress, tight but not too tight, with a row of buttons along the left side from shoulder all the way down. It wasn't a fancy dress, plain cotton. She'd left the bottom two buttons undone to show a flash of thigh when she moved. No slip. I liked that. She stepped over in tall black high heels, drawing her 5'6" frame closer to my six feet.

"I see you met the old one."

I saw the man standing now, head lowered as he looked at us.

"Professor Yog." Alizée patted my chest. "This is Lucien Caye." She looked at me. "The professor is descended from the old ones who came to earth eons ago and after a tragic war with other space travelers, survived by breeding with humans."

Yog blinked at me and said, "I am only part human."

"I hope it's the good part."

I'm not sure if it was a smile or a grimace but if the man wasn't a hunched geezer, I would have been reaching for my .45 automatic. He glided out of the room carrying a large book I hadn't seen him pick up. I say glided because his legs barely moved but he made good time crossing the room and out into the hall without looking back.

"What the hell was that?" I whispered.

She smiled up at me. "Professor Yog's a retired professor of antiquity from Miskatonic University. New England. Rhode Island, I think. He's been here for ten years looking for a distant relative called Sluggoth."

"Wha – "

"You know that swamp between Gentilly and Chef Menteur Pass?"

"Bayou Sauvage?"

"Sluggoth lives there or in the lagoon in Audubon Park."

"In the lagoon?"

She shrugged and turned and we went out to the car. I looked around for a green car, as I'd been doing regularly. Alizée sat close to me with her legs crossed and that dress opened to show me a few inches of her thighs, those sleek, shapely legs.

What I enjoyed with this girl were the silences. Riding with her without chatter, sitting with her without small talk. I waited for a streetcar to pass along Rampart, turned behind it and headed toward Canal Street and the Central Business District beyond, what the French called Faubourg Ste. Marie before the brash Americans bought the city and its people. Apparently my ancestors were already here, both sides of my family, according to my mother. I always wondered how they felt to be suddenly American.

"We're going uptown?" Alizée said as we meandered up Saint Charles Avenue in heavy traffic, the streetcars moving quicker next to us. I nodded and she looked out at the passing mansions of the Garden District. I turned up Washington Avenue and she seemed to relax a little and I realized she was tense. My parking luck held out and I found a parking place just down Claiborne from the restaurant.

"Ever eat here?" I took her hand as we passed below one of the neon signs that looked more like a movie marquee than a restaurant, one sign alongside the long, masonry building, one sign at the corner of the building. Each sign reached into the sky, vertical lettering, the one at the corner revolved: *T. Pittari's* in pink and *Restaurant* in green.

"The strangest restaurant in the city. Have you been here?"

She shook her head and we stepped into the place. The ceiling was low and the lights as well and the place smelled of sweet cooking fragrances. A middle-aged woman maitre d' checked my reservation and took us across a deep carpet to a small table near the center-right of the large dining room already crowded with mostly middle aged diners.

The waiters were older men. One with a pencil-thin moustache brought us menus and a wine list and told us his name was Herman and gave us the specialties of the day.

"Elk steak cooked over an open flame. Succulent and well seasoned. Eastern grey squirrel, oven roasted. Hammerhead shark baked with almond slices." A teen aged bus boy brought us water and a plate with several breads and a small tub of butter.

"Our breads this evening." Herman pointed them out. "Zwieback, a leavened sweet bread from Germany. It is crispy sweet. Massa Sovada, a Portuguese favorite made from milk, honey and sugar and Jamaican Bammy, flatbread made with coconut oil and coconut milk."

He bowed slightly. "I'll leave you to your menus."

Alizée leaned over her menu as a passing bus boy checked her out.

I told her, "All the meat here is wild game."

Under 'steaks' – the menu listed venison, buffalo (American bison), gazelle, kangaroo and elk. Under 'smaller cuts' – it listed Alpine marmot, nutria and eastern grey squirrel. Under fowl – it listed pheasant and Canadian goose. Under 'seafood' – it listed grouper, tiger shark, hammerhead and sting ray. Under 'exotic' – it listed rattlesnake, monitor lizard and tapir.

Under 'appetizer' was escargot, breaded quail strips, calamari and South China sea prawns.

We tried the prawns, which were oversized shrimp that came marinated and grilled. I tried slices of all three breads and saved the sweet Portuguese to eat as dessert.

Alizée remained quiet, stealing glances around the place.

"Hope you like your pheasant better than the prawns."

"I liked the prawns." She smiled back. "I just don't want to fill up." She looked around the room for the fourth time and the detective in me watched her as she kept her head down.

Her breast of pheasant was baked and served with Julianne potatoes. My rattlesnake meat came skewered on a shish-ka-bob with onion, red pepper and red potatoes. I expected the snake to be chewy. It wasn't. It tasted like lean chicken.

Restaurant owners Mr. and Mrs. Tom Pittari made their way through the tables, greeting customers. Bald headed Mr. Tom asked Alizée what she thought of the pheasant and she told him it was succulent.

"It's Asian pheasant from Russia."

Mrs. Pittari asked if I liked the snake. She was a chubby woman with a nice, warm smile.

"What kind of rattlesnake is it?"

"Western diamondback," Mr. Tom said. "Nobody fools with Eastern diamondbacks. Too damn mean and too damn poisonous."

Three men at the table behind Alizée kept staring our way after the Pittaris moved on. They were older men, late fifties maybe, in business suits. I was in a blue suit as well but left my tie at home.

I was going to ask Alizée if she didn't like the pheasant but the way she was surreptitiously looking around, I didn't think it was the food that had her clenched up. I'd decided on T. Pittari's because the food was exotic but it wasn't a fancy place. I didn't know how many fancy restaurants this girl had been to and I disliked the overpriced big restaurants this city was becoming famous for.

When the three men behind Alizée finished and walked past, one stopped and looked down at her and she looked up.

"Good to see you, dear." He smiled warmly, nodded to me and followed his friends out.

She let out a long breath, looked at her plate, speared a slice of pheasant. She brought it to her mouth but put the fork down. She looked at me, put her napkin on the table and asked where was the ladies room.

I pointed over her left shoulder to a side hall and stood as she left the table. She looked at no one, went straight into the hall. I glanced at my Bulova as I sat and looked it was twelve minutes later when she came out, walked straight to our table without looking around. She sat, looked at me with a wane smile.

"You OK?"

She nodded.

"Dessert?"

She shook her head. When Herman came I asked for a doggie bag, the check and left a nice tip.

Alizée took my hand on the way out but did not meet the eyes of anyone and several men and woman glanced at us as we passed, a nice young couple, I'm sure. No one leered, most paid no attention to us.

The air smelled of ozone and a damp breath of wind flowed over us before we climbed into the Ford. Rain on the way. It found us before we crossed Canal, Alizée sitting quietly close to me, looking out the side window.

"When we get to your place," she said. "I want to talk with you about something."

"I thought you might want to go dancing." I said with a smile.

She tried to laugh but it caught in her throat and her eyes looked damp.

I LET HER lead the way up to the apartment and to the sofa. Harri ran into the room and made a beeline to her as she sat and she scooped the little girl, pet her, the kitten meowing.

"Coffee, beer, whisky?"

"What kind of whisky?"

"Bourbon or scotch."

She shook her head and said, "Coffee."

It took the percolator a few minutes. I mixed two mugs full of coffee-and-chicory with cream and sugar, brought them to the coffee table. Alizée had been roughhousing with Harri, so much the kitten let out a 'Rowl' and rushed off when I sat down. She moved to the floor, sat and licked her fur back into place.

We each took a sip of coffee. Alizée put her cup on the coffee table, took my cup, put it next to hers and kissed me, kissed me again and her tongue touched mine and it came hot and frenzied, kissing, her pushing me back on the sofa, moving atop me, her left leg easing between my legs and the kissing continued until she pulled her mouth away, lifted her head.

"Any chance Jeannie will come in?"

"Kaye will keep her there. She knows we're going out tonight."

"And you'll probably bring me home." Her smile went away and she took in a deep breath, moved her body down to lay her head on my chest.

"Before I lose control," she said in a soft voice.

"Go ahead, lose control."

She sighed and I realized joking was not an option here.

"Before I fall more in love with Jeannie, I have to tell you something."

"Is it about those men in the restaurant?"

She looked up at me, wide eyed and nodded slowly, put her head back on my chest.

"I'm not a good girl, Lucien."

If there's one thing I've learned, when a woman is this serious. Shut up and listen.

"When my mommie died, we were living in a small place. Too small but I had a job. At Boudreaux's Grocery. I could pay the rent and I ate because Mrs. Boudreaux made sandwiches at the grocery and there was always some left over. A man came in one day and made me an offer. Like a business offer. He was an M.D., believe it or not, and could arrange dates for me where I could make money. He took no money. I kept it all. They were his friends. Professional men. Married. Mostly older men.

"I don't want to go into details, Lucien, but I've been saving money to start a new life. Only I can't leave New Orleans. No one can, can they? The Varennes changed my life, the old dears. They knew what I was up to and since I started working for them, for a year now, I haven't had to turn a trick."

Damn, I was getting soft. My throat was too tight for me to say anything.

I haven't had to turn a trick?

I pulled Alizée close and hugged her hard and felt her shake. Crying most likely and I held her. When she finally could control her voice, she said, "What I'm trying to say is you can let me be your girlfriend or bring me home and never see me again." She took in a breath. "If my Papa contacts you, I hope you will see me then."

I ran my hand down her back.

She waited, finally said, "Are you going to say anything?"

"I'm not about to let you go. If you think I'll ever judge you like that, think bad of you, well, you don't know me. I've slept around, Alizée. That's how Jeannie came about. Our problem was growing up Catholic. They pass out guilt with the host at mass, brainwash us that we have to confess sins."

I pulled her chin up to looked at her eyes.

"If you think I'm looking for the right virgin, you are mistaken. I prefer women with a touch of larceny."

"You're serious?"

"Stick around. You'll see."

She put her head back down and snuggled with me. Harri climbed on top of Alizée, curled up on her back and we stayed that way until morning light woke me. Sunlight streamed through the blinds, illuminating her face, soft, sleeping. Her breath fell on my neck. Her long, lustrous hair caught the light – auburn hair, many colored strands of brown and red and blond. Chestnut and burgundy.

She let out a sigh and I felt claws tap the top of my head. Harri came down and settled on the other side of my neck and we all went back to sleep.

WHEN THE DOORBELL buzzed Sunday night, I thought it might be Frenchy with the results of the firearms examination. Instead a tall man stepped into the foyer and looked at my office door. He heard me moving down the stairs and looked up.

Gray streaked his sandy hair. He was still thin, as Alizée described, stood an inch or so taller than me and wore a gray work shirt, black trousers and scuffed brown shoes. He held the envelope with 'Papa' on it in his shaky left hand, raised it as I stepped up.

"Are you Lucien Caye?" His French accent was heavy. Up close I saw a gaunt, unshaven face, dark circles around his light brown eyes. His clothes were baggy on his frame.

"Monsieur Diluviennes, I presume."

He nodded and I unlocked my office door, led him in.

"Would you like some coffee or something stronger?"

"Something stronger."

I went into the kitchen and drew down the bottle of Courvoisier that John Stanford had given me for Christmas a couple years back. It was still three-quarters full. I'm not much of cognac man but I figured a Frenchman would like it. I brought the bottle and a glass to my desk, nodded for him to sit and handed him the cognac.

He poured himself a double with shaking hands, took a hit as I sat in my captain's chair. Not sure it was a good idea giving him liquor. He was either a stone alcoholic or on something worse.

"My daughter. Will she see me?"

"Is that your message?"

"I would like to see my daughter."

"I'll tell her. In the morning. Where can we find you?"

He took another hit, shook his head, looked at the windows. The venetian blinds were closed.

"It is too dangerous."

"You're in danger?"

His head bobbed.

I shrugged, told him, "Danger is my business." *I think Philip Marlowe said that. No. He said, 'Trouble is my business'. I think.*

"You do not understand. Men are looking for me. Bad men."

"Dark skinned men with moustaches, one with a scar on his face?" I drew a line down my left cheek. I thought he would drop the glass. He put it on the desk, his hand shaking now, his face growing paler.

"You have seen them?"

"No. But they've been trying to find your daughter and you're not leaving until you tell me who the fuck they are."

He sat back.

"Who are they?" I got up, moved toward the windows, ready to cut him off if he bolted for the door. Having a nice-sized office gave me room to run down idiots. I looked back at him, waited.

"Have you ever heard of Unione Corse? La Mafia Francaise. The French Mafia?"

I shook my head and he finished his double, poured himself another and I moved over, picked up the bottle.

"They are after me. A misunderstanding." He sipped his cognac and gave me a quivering smile.

"What do you know about these two? Where are they staying?"

He shook his head.

"How long have you been in town?"

"I come in on *Zenora*. Spanish ship from Barcelona. Docked here March 2nd.

Six weeks ago. Damn.

I knew I had to get him away from my building, hoping he wasn't followed.

"Where are you staying?"

"I am on street."

"You can't come back here and you can't go where your daughter lives. If she wants to see you, I'll bring her to you." Had to think quickly. "The cathedral."

I stepped close, made sure he was paying attention. "Saint Louis Cathedral. Five thirty p.m. tomorrow. Sharp. We'll be inside. If we're not there, your daughter doesn't want to see you."

There was a six o'clock mass. People would be filing in. It wasn't the biggest cathedral but there were three doors in front, exits on each side and one in back, in case I had to take Alizée out quickly. Would French Mafiosi shoot up a Catholic cathedral? *How the fuck would I know?*

"Come on. You're leaving."

I thought of taking him out the side door, but no. If those two assholes followed him to the front door, let them follow him away from it. I slipped my .45 automatic into my belt at the small of my back and led him out of my office. I turned off the hall light and nodded to the door.

"Can you advance me a dollar? For food."

I took out my wallet, gave him a fiver. "Don't be late tomorrow."

He went out without thanking me and stood just outside the door, in the light and looked up and then down the street. I looked through the glass portion of the door, waiting for gunfire from the park across the street. Nothing. He turned to the left and moved slowly away. I locked the building door, raced down the hall for the side door, went out quickly, making sure it locked behind me.

He hadn't come down Dauphine or turned up, so he was still on Barracks and I spotted him not a half block away, same side of the street, heading toward the river. I followed, got away from the streetlight and crossed the street to tail him. He passed two men coming up the banquette and I reached back for my weapon but the men didn't even look at him. I overtook a couple, who gave me a wary look. This was the lower Quarter.

I expected him to turn into the nearest bar but Alizée's father surprised me, stepping into a small Mexican café when he reached Decatur Street. I found an alcove between two buildings where I could watch both doors and waited. A half hour crept by.

A group of four came out with Alizée's father right behind and he turned up Decatur, walking quicker now. I made the corner and spied him turn into an alcove. Was he watching to see who passed? I crossed the street, found another alcove and waited. My patience finally ran out and I crept up the street until I could see into his alcove. Empty. I crossed the street and found an open gate at the back of the alcove and rear patios where he'd made his escape.

No wonder he'd lasted all these weeks. He wasn't as fried as he looked.

It was too late to call Alizée, but I stayed focused, took a roundabout way back home, approaching my building up Burgundy Street. Cabrini Park loomed blacked out and I slipped inside and crossed the damp grass, moving from oak to magnolia tree to another oak. I checked out the brick and concrete WPA shelter, went into both bathrooms, but no one was around. When I stepped out of the women's bathroom, a movement caught my eye as a cat darted past too fast for me to see its color.

I moved in the darkness along the brick wall, looking at my building before going out on Dauphine Street to go back inside through the side door.

WHEN SHE STEPPED outside the next morning, I climbed out of my Ford and Alizée saw me, came over, moved right up and kissed me softly.

"Thought I'd give you a ride to work."

She had her hair tied back in a ponytail and wore a gray skirt and pale yellow blouse. I waited until we were in the car.

"Your father came by my office last night."

She took in a quick breath, those eyes searing mine.

"He wants to see you."

She just stared back.

"I told him we'd meet him at the cathedral at five thirty. If we're not there, you don't want to see him."

She looked at the windshield, blinked a couple times. I picked up her perfume now. She nodded. I made sure we weren't followed.

"Why the cathedral?"

I took her hand. "He's not in good shape, Alizée." I described him in detail but she showed nothing on her face, no reaction in her eyes.

"I'm sure those men looking for you are trying to find him. They're gangsters."

She nodded again and I started up the engine. Alizée said nothing all the way to work.

"I'll pick you up after work and we'll head straight there."

She leaned over and kissed me again. She climbed out and I thought of something and got out.

"What?"

"I'm making sure everything's OK in there."

She sighed, took out a key and we went in. Both Varennes were in and she checked with them, came back into the foyer and kissed me again.

"Go. We'll be OK."

MY PHONE RANG a minute after I stepped back into my office.

"Mr. Caye? This is your answering service. I have a message for you from Lieutenant Capdeville that came in fifteen minutes ago."

"Go ahead."

"I'll read it verbatim." It was Bobbie's sexy voice. "Lucy. Your fat friend is dead at his office. Come see." She paused a second. "Is he serious?"

"Yes, ma'am."

Serious? And he called me 'Lucy' too. *Jesus.*

A UNIFORMED COP, a heavy-set rookie with the name tag Truehart, stopped me right off the elevator on the fourth floor of the Carondelet Building, which was actually on Gravier Street, a block up from Carondelet Street and around the corner from old man Brienne's office in the Baronne Building. The hall was dark and smelled stale. The building was built around 1920 and yellowed light fixtures in the hall had never been replaced.

"Lt. Capdeville sent for me." I handed Truehart a card.

"Let him through," Frenchy called out as he stepped into the hall three doors from the elevator. He wore a gray suit, his curly hair hanging wild today. He tapped ashes from his cigarette to the carpet, put the butt back in his mouth and took a drag. He blew it out as I stepped up, smiling at me now.

"When did the ass-hole start calling you Lucy?"

"He told you? I thought you said he was dead."

"He is. He left you a note." Frenchy called for one of the detectives inside and Al Francona peeked out. Normally, the sharp-looking Italian smiled a lot. Not right now. Bodies tend to do that. He nodded at me and Frenchy asked him to bring out the note.

"It was under his desk," said Frenchy.

Al brought out a manila folder and Frenchy took it, opened it to show me a sheet of typing paper.

"It was in a sealed envelope with '909 Bar' scribbled in pencil on it."

909 Barracks Street. My address.

The note was typed:

'Lucy. Theirs more money to be gotten out of Mr. D. I'm being tailed so I'm sending this by messenger. Call me. I.A.'

'Theirs'. *A public school graduate.*

Frenchy closed the folder.

"Lucy?"

"Don't start or I'll tell everyone your name's spelled with an 'ie'." *The female spelling.*

He blew smoke in my face again.

"OK. Pretty Baby. Who the fuck's Mr. D?"

"André Diluviennes. I'm meeting him at five thirty. Saint Louis Cathedral." I gave the lieutenant the low down, describing the other men.

"Ever hear of the Unione Corse? French Mafia."

"Yeah, but not much."

"Mr. D thinks the two men I just described may be Unione Corse."

"Fuck." Frenchy dropped his cigarette on the hall carpet, stepped on it. "You said this Mr. D looked strung out. Like a dope fiend."

"Like a heroin addict."

Frenchy fired up another cigarette. "So your fat friend was being followed."

"Could be the men I just described."

Frenchy peeked into the office, told Francona he was headed to the bureau, told me to come along. "This is the 20th Century, Pretty Baby. Let's give Paris a call, see what the Sureté can tell us about this union."

A thin teen-ager with carrot red hair and wearing a white T-shirt and dungarees stood next to Truehart now.

"This guy says he's a bicycle messenger."

The teen looked at Frenchy. "I'm to pick up a package from Room 409."

Frenchy blew smoke in the kid's face.

"I'm a bicycle messenger. CBD Bike Service. I don't want any trouble." The kid held up a notebook, flipped it open, read from it. "Call came at six-thirty last night from a Mr. Accalula. Pick up was for ten a.m. I'm a little early."

"Actually, you're late. Your client's dead."

"Damn. Was he, like, you know. Murdered?"

Frenchy nodded.

The kid looked at me and bounced on his toes and said, "Just like in the movies."

"We're looking for a teen-ager with red hair," Frenchy said and the kid went pale. Frenchy stepped past him, patted him on the shoulder and said, "Just screwing with you kid."

He told Truehart to take the kid to Francona so his statement could be taken.

At least Frenchy put out his cigarette before we got into the elevator.

"How'd he get it?"

"Three in the chest. One in the head. Fuckin' place was ransacked. Looks like it happened last night."

"Who found him?"

"Sixty year old cleaning woman. This morning."

Only good news out of this, I thought. If those assholes were Unione Corse and saw the envelope, they should be looking for a bar called 909. Good they aren't from the city.

"Any news on the gun I turned into you?"

"What gun?"

THE FRENCH INSPECTOR's name was Valery Michel Lamy, sounded pretty old on the phone, spoke English with a heavy accent. Frenchy handed me the phone, said the accent was giving him a headache. I put the inspector on hold and moved into the squad room. No way I could stay in Frenchy's smoky office. It took three hours and six phone calls back and forth before I had everything the Sureté could give me for now.

Between calls, detectives meandered around, the ones who knew me came to poke me, drop rubber-bands on my head, toss pencils as they went back and forth to the coffee pot. On the wall above the coffee pot, some clown had put up an art-deco painting of a vulture perched above a gold NOPD Detective's badge with a slogan – NOPD HOMICIDE. It was a nice painting actually.

I stood just outside the door of Frenchy's small office and read him the pertinent information from the Sureté –

"The Unione Corse started in Corsica and is centered on the mainland in Marseilles now. They began as strong-arm thugs but now they control the heroin distribution." I looked up at Frenchy. "Throughout Europe."

"Damn."

I went back to my notes. "They worked with the French Resistance during the war, killed Nazi sympathizers, broke up strikes after the war, joined the local Gendarmerie, which helped them organize their heroin empire. They've been importing opium from Laos and Vietnam by ship. They are establishing smuggling routes from Marseilles to New York and New Orleans."

"Fuck."

"They never heard of any Diluviennes and have no information on who's involved in the New Orleans operation but Inspector Lamy is contacting police in Lyon for help. Apparently no cops south of Lyon can be trusted when it comes to the Unione Corse, from Bordeaux all the way to Marseilles."

I looked at him again. "Apparently these fucks are as ruthless as the Mafia. Corsicans. Sicilians. Jesus."

"I heard the Sardinians are pretty fuckin' mean too."

"The Unione Corse has a symbol. A Moor's head. An African man with a rag tied around his forehead."

I told Frenchy I left his number and my office number with Lamy.

He nodded, said he'd be at the cathedral later about this Mr. D.

I told him I needed to talk to the man first. "His daughter will be with me. She's my client."

"What?"

"Family matter. Then you can have him."

"You tellin' me what to do now?"

"With this. Yeah. You just keep an eye out for a pair of heavy-set, olive-skinned slugs with moustaches, one with a scar on his left cheek." I backed away from the door. "And a green car."

He grinned at me, shot me the bird.

I PICKED UP Alizée early and parked behind the cathedral on Orleans Avenue. We took Pirate Alley past Saint Anthony's Garden with its obelisk built for some French sailors who died during one of our yellow fever epidemics. Huge magnolia trees hovered over the white statue of Jesus with His arms open in the garden. We stepped around to the front of Saint Louis Cathedral and went inside. I led her half way up the center aisle and into the pews, settling next to a pillar where we could sit half hidden and watch the doors.

Alizée hadn't said a word since I picked her up.

Several women in black knelt up front. Could have been the same women from Saint Alphonsus. Tourists came in the back and looked around, admiring the stain-glassed windows, huge chandeliers, magnificent altar up front with frescos, the statues of Saint Louis, King of France and Joan of Arc in golden armor at the rear. I thought of going up to the balustrade but we had several good escape routes where we sat.

I spied Frenchy Capdeville move in to sit in a back pew. Detective Al Francona came in a minute later to sit across the aisle in another back pew. As five-thirty rolled past, people began to come in for mass. Alizée decided looking around was more interesting than staring at the floor. I'd noticed she didn't bother with the holy water when we came in, didn't even genuflect before we moved into the pews. Neither did I, but I've had bad experience with holy water. I tend to contaminate it if I dipped my fingers inside. Didn't mind polluting it at Saint Alphonsus, but not here at the cathedral.

I was getting a little worried as more people came in and it was closing in on six p.m. Frenchy went out to smoke, I'm sure, and when he came back in he was followed by three more women in black and André Diluviennes. He wore the same clothes but he'd managed to shave and run a comb through his hair.

I waited for him to look our way and took Alizée's hand and slid out from behind the pillar, nodding to him as I drew

Alizée to the side aisle. He came around and started our way and I moved us beyond the confessional box and waited in the small alcove next to the side door that opened to Pirate Alley.

Alizée squeezed my hand as her father came into view. He stopped and stared at her and tears welled in his eyes. She squeezed my hand harder.

His lips quivered as he spoke in French, a low voice and I heard *Mon Dieu* (My God) and *beau* (beautiful).

"English, Papa. Speak in English." She wiped a tear from her eye.

"You are the most beautiful thing I have ever seen."

I eased back but was still between them.

He started shaking his head, looked down a moment, then looked up. "Alizée. Allie. My beautiful daughter." He opened his hands. "Your Papa is a bum. I am no good. I never was good, except when I was here." He looked up at the ceiling for a second. "Here in New Orleans. But I destroyed that, did I not?"

She nodded, wiped another tear away.

"Your mama." He shook his head again and tears rolled down his face. I spied Frenchy and Francona move into the pews behind and sit.

"I know she is gone."

"Yes, Papa. Gone." Alizée's voice was a little stronger.

He tried to smile. "I am so glad you let me see you one more time." He straightened his back. "I have a cancer and the doctors say I have not long to live. I came to see you."

Alizée nodded slowly, her lips pressed tight.

"I do not ask forgiveness for my evil. I destroy everything. I do not say this to be felt sorry for. It is my fault."

"Yes, Papa. It is."

He smiled sadly now and dug into his pants pocket. He pulled out a small brown pouch, unwrapped it and came out with a gold chain with a blue gemstone in a pendant.

"It is only a sapphire," he said. "But it is of excellent quality." He showed it to her. "I buy it from the finest jeweler in Geneva. Switzerland. I carry this a long time." He held it out to her. "I want to give you something to remember that even a father who is a bum can love his daughter."

He inched closer, holding it up higher and Alizée's eyes were locked on his. He put it around her neck and fixed the clasp. He kissed her cheeks softly.

"May I hug you?"

Her eyes were filled now and she nodded and the man hugged his little girl and I stepped into the aisle behind them. I waved Frenchy over, mentioned to him he might want to put a man in Pirate Alley in case Mr. D decided to go out the side door.

"I have two patrolmen out there and in front too."

Bells rang and a priest started up the aisle with two altar boys and walked up to the altar to begin mass. Ushers came up both side aisles. Ours was a man in his fifties in a black suit. He whispered we needed to sit.

Frenchy opened his coat to show his badge and revolver.

The usher looked at me.

"I'm with him."

He went around us and I looked at Alizée in time to see her father go out the side door. My head snapped back to Frenchy who came past us and went out the door.

Alizée asked, "Who's that?"

"Police. I'll explain in a minute." I took her hand and tried to guide her back up the aisle to leave through the front of the cathedral, but she pulled me toward the side door. I held her back a moment. No gunshots so we went out.

Frenchy had a hand on her father's arm and was directly him down the alley to Chartres Street, with a patrolman in front and one behind.

"What is happening?"

"Your father has information the police need."

She looked at me.

"The fat man hired by your father to find you. He was murdered this morning."

She let out a squeak, grabbed my hand again, looked at her father.

"They know your father didn't kill anyone." I wasn't sure about that statement, but I stuck to it.

"The other men searching for you. They were probably looking for your Papa."

"Why?"

I told her I didn't know.

"Then my Papa is in danger."

"He's safe for now with the police." I pulled on her hand for her to look up at me. "You are not safe Alizée, until we find these men."

JOHN STANFORD MIGHT have been in his eighties, but the man's mind was as sharp as a twenty year old and I sometimes wondered if he wasn't a cop, maybe even a detective back in England at the turn of the century. He brought out his old Webley .38 revolver with its five-inch barrel, blue steel finish, one of those revolvers with a top-breaking cylinder. He kept it well oiled. I'd bought him fresh ammo about four months ago.

"I might be a while," I told him.

"I'll keep an eye on the place," he assured me, standing in his doorway with a maroon smoking jacket and black slacks, brown slippers.

Hold Me, Babe

Alizée and Jeannie were locked in our apartment across the hall. They were watching TV and playing with Harri with one of her favorite toys. One of my old socks, which the kitten found and dragged out from under the couch. I checked right away and it was a clean sock, at least, before giving Harri back her kill.

Before I stepped out, Alizée came over and looked up at me.

I kept my voice low. "The police are finished with your Papa. I thought I'd pick him up, take him home. I'd like to know where he's staying."

She just looked at me.

"Do you want to see your Papa again?"

She shook her head, grabbed my left hand, squeezed it, pulled away before I could kiss her.

I made sure the building's doors were locked before exiting the side door to creep around front. The night shift tomcat was on the hood of my Ford. It was darker out tonight with the clouds. I crossed to the park to stand in the shadows next to the wall for a few minutes, letting my eyes adjust, looking for any movement.

The tomcat stood and stretched, arched his back, gave me a long stare as I approached the car and casually jumped off. I checked under the hood, then rode around the block looking for a green car before tooling over to the Detective Bureau. André Diluviennes was about to be released and I asked Frenchy to keep him there. I'd drive him off.

Frenchy was gone by the time I stepped into the bureau and Francona looked whipped.

Mr. D shoved the last piece of a sandwich into his mouth, washed it down with an RC Cola. At least they fed him.

"He's all yours." Francona yawned, leaned back in his chair and closed his eyes.

I'd parked in the NO PARKING zone next to the Coroner's Office morgue entrance along South White Street and looked around as Mr. D and I approached the Ford. He was oblivious to everything, almost walked past. I grabbed his arm, unlocked the front passenger door and he climbed in.

I took evasive maneuvers, circling back on our trail, taking my time to make sure we weren't tailed. In the quiet car his breathing was louder, labored, sounding dry.

He stared out the front windshield without expression as I headed on Tulane Avenue toward the river, figuring he's been hiding in the Quarter or Marigny. Stopping for a red light, I asked him where to.

"Toulouse Street Wharf."

Wharves were good places to hide. Why not?

I went all the way down to North Peters through medium traffic, watching the mirrors, looked for any green car. A left on Peters, I made a quick right at Saint Louis Street and headed straight down to the wharf. The lights along the far side of the wharf, far brighter than the streetlights, showed two ships being loaded.

"*Maraba*," he said as I eased up to a parking spot this side of the Toulouse Street Wharf Warehouse.

"Huh?"

"*SS Maraba*. Brazilian ship." He looked out at the warehouse and the towering masts of the ships beyond. "The captain is French. A childhood friend. He will take me away." He looked at me with sad eyes. "I am grateful to you. To see my Alizée. I have missed her. Terribly." His eyes began to fill.

"You really have cancer?"

"Oh, yes." He looked out at the ship's masts again. "I may not even make it to Brazil." He gritted his teeth, sucked in a hard breath.

He looked at me again. "Are you and my daughter, um, involved?"

"Just starting to get involved, Monsieur Diluviennes."

"Do not break her heart as I did."

"I won't."

He seemed to focus on me now as he stared. "You sound, um, sure, sure of yourself."

I took out my wallet, dug out the bills in there, handed them to him.

"Here. It's all the cash I have on me." Three tens, two fives, three ones. Forty three dollars.

He looked at the money, reached a shaking hand to take it.

"Thank you, monsieur."

He climbed out and went into the warehouse. I waited a half hour and never saw him again.

I COULD NOT remember the last time the four sets of lights outside the Third Precinct had no bulbs out. The brown brick building with its arched doors and windows, sat across Chartres Street from the towering, white Louisiana Supreme Court Building. I found a parking spot just up from the Napoleon House as a line of black NOPD prowl cars were parked. I timed it perfectly, a half hour before roll call.

"Hey, Hey. You slummin' or what?"

I turned to Kirk Eckland's voice as he climbed out of a car. Time to knock off.

"Got something for y'all." I handed him a copy of the description of the two olive skinned men I had typed out for the lieutenants to read at roll call. The sheet included my address and Alizée's boarding house to keep an eye on. This is what we called a patrol request.

"Remember the fat man I mentioned?" I said.

"Yeah."

"Ian fuckin' Allacula." Eckland spit on the pavement.

"He was murdered this morning."

"No shit?"

"I think it was the olive men."

I went in to pass the description to the outgoing and incoming shift lieutenants and to put the script up on the bulletin board.

MY SOFA WAS made up with sheets and one of the pillows from my bed. Alizée sat curled up on the easy chair in the semi-darkness with the radio on and Muddy Waters singing *Rollin' Stone*. She'd taken out her ponytail, her hair hanging in loose waves. The yellow blouse was pulled out and she was barefoot.

"My Papa?"

"He's taking a ship to Brazil."

"When?"

"He's on it now." I moved to the refrigerator, took out a couple bottles of Canadian lager I picked up at the wine cellar when I bought another six pack of Wells Bombardier for John. I popped the caps and stepped back into the living room.

"Jeannie stay up late?"

"Of course. She just went down. She wore Harri out."

She looked at the beer I handed her.

"What's this?"

"Moosehead beer. Light and smooth. From Canadia."

"You mean Canada."

"Aren't Canadians from Canadia?"

She gave me a weak smile, took a sip of beer.

"I want to take my songs to Edward Courant."

I leaned against the arm of the easy chair and she pulled me into it and we fit, squashed up, half her left leg in my lap.

"The Varennes know Courant. They say he's honest, although not much of a firecracker."

"Honest counts," I said.

"My songs will speak for themselves. If they're any good, any artist will be able to see."

"Could you sing one for me?"

She took another hit of beer. So did I. The Moosehead was light and bracing.

"I'm not a performer. My voice doesn't have the range but I'll sing one for you."

I waited.

"Not now, silly." She poked my shoulder. "I need my guitar or a piano."

We spent a few minutes in silence, finishing our beers and I took the bottles back into the kitchen.

"I'll take you to Courant tomorrow. You get a lunch break, don't you?"

I sat on the sofa and started taking off my shoes.

She stood and stretched.

"I have an extra toothbrush. I'll show you. And I'll take the sofa."

"But – "

"Ask Jeannie. Ladies never sleep on the sofa in the Caye house. My daughter took my bed until we got one for her."

"Ladies?"

"I've had a number of clients. Kaye as well after I found her and her baby out in the park. Single mom. I gave her the whole place, went and slept downstairs on the Chipping Bubbly.

"Ladies?" She smiled at me.

"Yes. A few clients I didn't want to sleep with."

"And the ones you wanted to sleep with?" She tip-toed over to me, a smarty-pants now.

"They kept calling me 'God' for some reason."

She laughed, covered her mouth, looked to the bedrooms in case she'd wakened Jeannie.

Up to me now, she moved her lips to mine, stopped, took in a breath.

"One kiss."

"Just one?"

"Please. If we start smooching heavily, I won't be able to stop."

I squinted at her. Almost said – *what's wrong with that.*

"It's up to me?"

"Yes." Her breath brushed my lips.

"You're serious."

"Yes."

"Let's save the kiss until after we brush our teeth. I don't like kissing women with beer breath."

She knuckled my chest.

IT WASN'T RAIN exactly, more mist or as Jeannie called it – "Wet air."

We sat at the small antique table next to the French doors in my living room as the sky darkened and went over her homework.

"You sure Alizée can't come over?"

My daughter was still in her school uniform, white button blouse and navy blue skirt, white socks and black flat shoes. This was the same uniform the girls wore when I went to Cathedral Academy right here in the Quarter. We boys wore khakis. It wasn't until tonight did I remember Jeannie told me she had gone to kindergarten at Saint Alphonsus.

"Was Father Callan the pastor when you were in kindergarten?"

She shrugged, told me she never saw a priest there. Or just didn't remember.

"You *sure* Alizée can't come over and help me with this?"

"She's busy."

"Doing what?"

"Working on her songs. She needs some time alone, you know."

"Why?"

I just gave her a long look.

"Come on. One more assignment." I picked up the small book.

"Alizée can do it better, you know."

"Do what?"

"My homework with me."

Harri decided the venetian blinds needed climbing and leaped from the table to the blinds of the window next to the French doors and scrambled to hang on while they swung with her.

"Rowl, meow." She looked at me and Jeannie reached over and disentangled the little tyke.

I opened the book. *Brer Rabbit.* Son-of-a-gun. I knew this story.

"Come on, We'll read it together." I moved to the sofa and Jeannie brought the kitty along, sat close to me and I opened the book across both of our laps. Jeannie read and I helped with the big words and wound up reading most of it, which I expected. Harri swatted the pages as we turned them.

Jeannie thought the tar baby was yucky.

"Why didn't the rabbit notice it was made of tar and couldn't answer him?"

"Rabbits aren't as smart as people, or foxes."

We read on as Brer Rabbit lost his temper with the tar baby that wouldn't answer him and hit it with a paw, then another until all four paws were stuck in tar. Jeannie did not expect the ending and liked it very much, as I had when I was little.

"So rabbits are pretty smart, after all," she said. "OK. All done." She put Harri down and assembled her books and notebooks. "Let's see what's on TV."

"Get in your pajamas and I'll make popcorn and we'll check out the TV."

Rain peppered the French doors as Jeannie sat on the sofa with the popcorn bowl and I went through the three channels. Shows were just coming on.

"Stop, Daddy. Let's watch this one."

Oh, no. The title made me cringe. *Martin Kane, Private Eye.*

It was worse than I thought but Jeannie stared intently as a pipe-smoking PI, hired by a hippy dame with a mink coat, tried to unravel the mystery of the missing ventriloquist and I couldn't help wonder why anyone would want to find a ventriloquist. If the bastard was lost, leave him lost or you might have to hear his routine.

"I'm glad you don't smoke, Daddy. Ralph smoked."

Ralph was the man Jeannie's mother married before she dropped our daughter on my doorstep.

"You should wear a hat sometimes."

"Why?" I munched more popcorn.

"I think you'd look nifty keen with a hat."

Nifty keen? At least my little girl thinks her old man could look nifty keen.

The commercials in this program were different. Sponsored by the U.S. Tobacco Company, instead of cutting away for commercials, ole Martin Kane seemed to find himself in his favorite tobacco shop to discuss pipe tobaccos and cigarettes with the tobacconist. Never heard of a tobacconist before. After refilling his pipe with a different blend, Kane went back to tracking the missing ventriloquist.

I tossed a popcorn on the coffee table and Harri jumped over and swatted it to the floor and pounced.

"I like Alizée a lot, Daddy. Do you like her?"

"Of course."

"I mean. Like her like a girlfriend. You know. Kissing."

I looked at her, said, "Twas brillig."

I like it when my daughter's eyes light up when I surprise her.

"And the slimy toads did gimble on the wave, whatever."

She laughed so hard, I had to grab the popcorn bowl. Harri came back to see what was up.

"Twas brillig," she said when she caught her breath, "and the slithy toves did gyre and gimble in the wabe."

"Right." I ate more popcorn.

She did too, then said, "You can only distract me with *Jabberwocky* for a minute." She pulled the hair on my arm. "Do … you … like … Alizée?"

I put a finger over my lips. "Shush. Don't tell her."

"Why not?"

"A boy has to tell a girl he likes her himself."

Her nose crinkled and she tossed a popcorn into her mouth.

"Is that how it works?"

"Sometimes. Sometimes nothing works."

She thought about that a few seconds, said, "You must have liked my mommie."

"Yes. But I went off to the war and she found someone else. It happened a lot."

We'd had this talk before, but she was just checking again. I found kids do that a lot. I told her I never would have missed the first years of her life if I'd known about her. She said she knew that. Her mommie told her I would be surprised to learn I had a daughter.

"Do you wish you had a son instead?"

"No."

"Why not?"

"Because I couldn't do this with a boy." I grabbed her face and kissed her cheek and forehead and nose and other cheek and chin and she squirmed, laughed.

The buzzer stopped me and Jeannie picked up a napkin and wiped her face.

"I didn't slobber your face," I said.

I hit the buzzer and went out to see who I'd buzzed in. A streak of smoke preceded Frenchy Capdeville into the foyer. I told Jeannie I was going down to the office and wouldn't be long.

"I'll tell you what happens on the case." She pointed to the TV.

I scooped Harri up before she could escape into the hall, passed her back to Jeannie and went downstairs.

Frenchy was about to toss his cigarette on the floor and I asked him to hold it for the ash tray.

I went straight to the refrigerator, popped two Falstaffs and we sat at either end of the Chipping Bubbly. We put our feet up on the coffee table and started drinking.

"Nothing on your olive-skinned men so Francona's going nutzo with an unsolved on his hands."

I told him about Mr. D and the ship to Brazil.

He just nodded and took a hit, then said, "About that gun."

"What gun?"

I waited as he took another hit of beer, smacked his lips, said, "The gun that's now at the bottom of the Mississippi."

"Oh, that one."

Frenchy nodded. "I had to wait for the right firearms examiner. And yes, it was the murder weapon."

I fuckin' knew it.

We both took a hit and Frenchy started shaking his head. "Alvin Haverton wasn't so stupid after all. He waited. Longer than I would have. Waited until it was all lined up. The moon, the stars, our captain laid up in the hospital, me out of town, Mrs. Slushy out with her lover boy and Haverton in line to catch the next murder case."

A car's brakes squealed outside and I waited for a crash. Nothing. I wondered if maybe a cat just got run over. I hoped not. So we sat there and finished our beers and eventually Frenchy got up and stretched.

"It's over," he said. "Tell your rich clients it was the guy in prison after all."

He started out and was surprised I followed. I told him about the cats and if one was squashed in the street, I would have to bury it. I'm a good neighbor.

"Open your hood."

"Why?"

"Kittens."

With the new light bulbs Kaye had put in under the balcony and the streetlight at the corner, the street was fairly lit up. No dead cat, thankfully and no kitten under the car's hood. Frenchy went around to climb into his black car. He waited for me to look at him.

"Stay away from Mrs. Haverton and her daughter," he said. "We're never to talk of this again." As if I didn't know how cops worked when it came to one of us, especially a dead one of us.

"I've already forgotten."

"Good." He got in and drove off.

It was cool outside and I took in the night air for a few moments. As I turned to go back in, I saw a flash of white across the street. A cat, slim and moving softly on light paws, a mackerel striped and white cat on the banquette next to the wall. Harri's mom? It stopped and looked ahead. The cat on the night shift, my large, black and white friend trotted up to the white cat and they touched noses and both jumped up on the fence and leapt down into Cabrini Playground.

Had to admit, Harri's mom was a fine looking feline.

WHEN I STEPPED into my office from dropping off Alizée at work, my office phone rang.

"Detective Caye. This is Father Callan. They came back."

"When?"

"Just now. I got their license plate number."

"They're gone?"

"Yes. I uh, uh. Was I supposed to try to keep them?"

"No, Father. I'll be right there."

The priest was out in front of his church again, bouncing as I stepped up. He had a slip of paper in his hand.

"I made sure I got the number right. I think they saw me."

"The same two?"

"Yes. And the car is a green Chevrolet. Two-door."

"What did they say?"

"Only the one with the scar spoke to me. He wanted to know if I found out about Wanda Murphy's daughter and her ex-husband. I told them no. He looked mad."

"What were they wearing?"

"The driver didn't get out. The man with the scar wore a black shirt and gray trousers."

"Which way did they go?"

He pointed downtown. "I watched them go straight up Constance and they didn't turn off."

I thanked him and started away.

"Wait. Can you tell me what the hell's going on?"

"Hell? You got it right padre. Those men are French Mafia. Next time you see them, call the police right away."

THE DETECTIVE BUREAU smelled of burned coffee and stale cigarette smoke. Al Francona opened a window as I stepped in and Frenchy waved me to his office. I stayed just outside and peered through the smoke as the lieutenant told me the license plate on the Chevy was a stolen plate.

"Doug's Used Car Lot on Claiborne. Plate was on a black Dodge. Doug didn't even know the plate was missing." He put out his latest cigarette as Francona stepped up next to me.

"We got an APB out on the car and plate."

"Did you show him the pictures?" Francona said.

I had to go into the smoke room as Frenchy dug out four telex photoprints.

"From the Sureté. These are the known Union Corse gangsters with scars on their faces."

Swarthy looking bastards. They must recruit only ugly Frenchmen.

"This one's got a scar on the left side of his face."

"So."

Francona suggested we go together to show Father Callan.

I rode with him in an unmarked black Ford that looked identical to mine only it rattled and sputtered when he gave it the gas.

"So Diluven – whatever the fuck his name is – took a ship out of port."

"*SS Maraba* sailed this morning."

"Wish he'd have stayed to bait these killers. They're looking for him, right?"

"Unfortunately they think his daughter can lead them to him."

Francona leaned on his horn as a white Mercury ran a stop sign in front of us.

"She's a looker, the daughter."

I just nodded.

"Little young for you, wouldn't you say?"

"Six years younger."

"Jesus. I thought she was a teen-ager."

"That's what you get from thinking, pisano."

"Yeah? Well you don't have an unsolved murder to work."

I looked at him until he looked back.

"You think I'm not working this with you?"

He didn't seem impressed. I let it lay there until we reached Constance Street and told him Alizée wasn't just a client and I wasn't slowing down until we caught the two thugs.

Father Callan picked the man with the scar out right away, bouncing again as we stood outside Saint Alphonsus. The name under the photo was Joseph Darnand, age thirty-eight.

"I'll get this out to everyone," Francona said.

When we got back to the bureau, I had a copy of Darnand's photo made for me.

FOR TWO DAYS she had come and sat under the WPA shelter in the park across from my office with her baby, sometimes rocking the infant, sometimes walking between the oaks and magnolias, back and forth. Sometimes she would sing. She came around nine a.m. and around lunchtime she'd reach into the paper bag she'd brought and nibble on a sandwich. After, she would cover her shoulder with a small pink blanket and nurse her baby beneath the blanket. Around five p.m., she would walk away, up Dauphine Street.

On the third morning the rain swept in, one of those all-day New Orleans rainstorms that started suddenly then built into monsoon proportions. The newspaper said to expect showers brought in by an atypical autumn cool front from Canada, which would finally break the heat wave that has lingered through the sizzling summer of 1948. I grabbed two umbrellas and found her huddled under the shelter.

"Come on," I told her, "come get out of the rain – "

THAT'S HOW I met Kaye Rudabaugh three years ago. She trusted me enough to come in and I help her and future husband Charley out of a jam. Kaye reminded me of my mother. Maybe it was the song she sang to baby Donna, probably still sings it. In French, my mother sang it to me when I was little. The refrain went, "The heart has reasons of which reason knows nothing."

I've never known a truer statement.

All this came to mind when Kaye carried Donna and Charley followed them into the apartment for Jeannie's birthday party. John Stanford was already there in a blue smoking jacket and sipping a Wells Bombardier. Jeannie rushed out of the bedroom with Harri, Alizée right behind.

My daughter wore a new blue dress that reminded me of the one Alice wore in the movie. Alizée's hair was fly-away, fluffy and looked darker today, more like red-brick. She wore matching lipstick and looked so damn sexy in a slimming gray sweater dress that hugged her body. She came to me, reached up and brushed my lips with hers so softly I'm sure she left no lipstick, and went into the kitchen to the cake sitting on the table.

Charley patted me on the back as we joined the girls. He stood about five-ten with curly light brown hair and green eyes. He'd been filling out a little recently. Married life.

"How old are you now?" Charley called out.

"Eight." Jeannie pointed to her cake. "Count the candles."

Alizée lit the candles and we sang *Happy Birthday* and Jeannie blew out the candles. I was going to help with the cake and ice cream but Kaye shooed us away and Charley had to hurry to catch Donna who chased Harri into the living room.

The cake was sickly-sweet white with white frosting. At least the ice cream was chocolate. We assembled in the living room for Jeannie to open her presents. Donna helped, ripping the wrappings while Harri flailed at the loose paper and hid under it.

Jeannie opened Alizée's present first. A record album, the soundtrack of songs from *Alice in Wonderland*, which she took right over to the Philco. Alizée followed, showed her there was an added track of a man reciting *Jabberwocky*.

She opened my present next and cried out when she saw it was a stuffed Cheshire cat.

"How'd you find that?" Alizée asked.

"I'm a detective, aren't I?"

My daughter wasn't as interested in the fifty dollar saving bond I gave her because I told her it went into a safe deposit box in the bank. "You're getting one each birthday and Christmas from now on. One day you'll have a chunk of money."

John's present was next, a vintage doll from England.

"Her name's Edwina," he said. "She's rather homely. I think it supposed to make little girls feel better about themselves. Unless the little girl's uglier."

Alizée thought this was funny as hell, while Jeannie smiled and showed Donna the doll and the three-year old slapped it. I tried not to laugh but the doll was hideous. John beamed.

The Rudabaughs's present consisted of two containers of something called silly putty. While they demonstrated how it could lift newsprint from a newspaper, I went into my bedroom closet for Jeannie's last present. When I stepped into the living room, she jumped up and squealed.

"A hula hoop!"

She took it out of my hand and moved to the open area in front of the TV.

"What is it?" John asked.

She showed him, swinging it around her hips and moving her hips to keep it up.

"That's it?" John asked me.

"That's it."

Jeannie let Donna try the hula hoop but the little one just watched it spin twice and fall to the floor. Alizée came out of the bedrooms with another present and handed it to Jeannie who brought it to me.

"I've never given you a birthday present."

I almost said it wasn't my birthday but the smile on her face told me to keep quiet and open it. It looked like a hat box. It was and inside was a black fedora.

"Private Eyes wear hats on TV."

I stood, went to the mirror next to the Philco, put on the fedora and turned back. A fedora all right but with brim wasn't a wide one and that was good.

Jeannie clapped. Alizée winked at me and I moved to the sofa and watched Donna try to reach for the swinging hula hoop while *The Caterpillar Song* came on the soundtrack. Alizée sat next to me.

"What's the matter?" she asked.

"What makes you think something's the matter?"

"Your face."

"Oh."

I took her hand, watched my little girl laughing and swinging the hula hoop again.

"What?" Alizée prodded me with an elbow.

I kept it low. "Just thinking of all those young birthdays I missed."

"You won't miss anymore." She smiled sadly and I realized I was talking to someone whose father walked away from more than just birthdays. She got up and asked Jeannie for the hula hoop and Alizée had no problem keeping it up, moving smoothly as the hoop rose to her breasts, then back down to her waist and her hips and back up, the hoop rolling across that sweater dress.

Charley caught my eyes and let his eyebrows go up and down. John sat next to me, watching her as well. A devious smile came to Alizée's face as she stared at me, swinging her hips around, raising her arms.

John poked my shoulder. "I say. I think I do like it. What? Ho?"

THE LONG WHITE Cadillac pulled up outside, parked behind my Ford and the six foot, lean chauffeur with the pock-marked face came in. His uniform was different. Powder blue now, the color of Field Marshal Herman Goering's ridiculous uniform without the gold braid or the iron cross medals. He crossed my office with another envelope in hand.

He glanced past my shoulder and flinched.

"I thought that was a statue."

I felt Harri's claws as the little girl, who'd be sitting up on the bookshelf behind me, decided she preferred my shoulder. I got up, peeled her off my shirt and put her on the desk before going around to take the envelope.

The chauffeur backed away from the desk as Harri came toward him. He watched the kitten carefully.

"I don't like cats."

"It's not a cat. Yet. It's a kitten."

He stood about ten feet from the desk, backed up some more as Harri reached the end of the desk and sat looking at him. I opened the unsealed envelope and pulled out another piece of Brienne cream-colored stationery.

Typed again:

Dear Lucien,
Call me when you can to set up an appointment so I may pick up the report on your investigation.

Sincerely,
Angél Brienne

She added her phone number, as if I didn't know it.

"She sent you instead of just calling?"

"Miss Brienne distrusts answering services."

She must have called.

Harri raised a paw and swatted the air.

"If it jumps on me, I'll slap it across the room."

The man was twenty feet away now. How far did he think a kitten could jump? His mouth frowned and his fists were clenched. I scooped Harri.

"Slap my kitten and I'll break your fuckin' jaw."

"Cats and I don't get along."

"Well I have her under control. You got anything else for me?"

He looked at me now. "I don't like being threatened."

"Then don't come back, smiley."

He backed toward the door and didn't turn until he was almost there, as if I'd sic Harri on him. She was too busy licking my fingers. He left and I went to the window, watched the Caddy pull away. The engine was too hot for a kitten to climb on and he didn't run over anything.

Douche bag.

I spent the afternoon typing a report for Angél and found writing fiction more entertaining than my usual reports.

I WENT BACK to Cypress Grove Cemetery, found Sammy patching up a concrete tomb near the center of the place. He gave me a wary look when I stepped up.

"Remember me?"

"Yes, I do."

I pulled out a twenty this time, put it on the tomb's ledge. The tomb was marked *Laurent* with five names of New Orleanians interred between 1846 and 1933.

"There are some bad men looking for the daughter of the woman I asked about, Wanda Murphy."

"How bad?"

"Murderers. Should be Frenchmen with heavy accents." I pulled the telex photo from my thin leather portfolio, showed him the face of Joseph Darnand.

He wiped his hands on his overalls, looked at the photo. "Damn."

"I'm not asking you to do anything. No hero shit trying to find out anything about them. Just don't give them the name of who pays for the perpetual care and her address. I found the daughter that way and they can too."

"Foreigners probably don't know about perpetual care," he said. "I'll make sure they don't find out."

I handed him a business card in case he needed to call me and pointed to the twenty.

"Thanks," I said and left it there.

I spotted a man duck behind a tomb and pulled out my .45. I had on my fedora that shielded my eyes from the bright sun as I stood behind one of the tall oaks, the walled tombs to my right, Sammy behind me, the stranger straight ahead.

"What's up?" Sammy whispered.

I raised my .45 and nodded ahead. "Someone's there."

Patience. I'd learned patience as a Ranger. Lying in wait for the enemy with my heart stammering. So I waited a good five minutes before the stranger came from around the tomb. He was short, medium build, took off his hat to run a handkerchief across his bald head. He was an elderly man who wiped his eyes with the handkerchief now. He wandered away. A distraught man in a cemetery.

He didn't have eyes in the back of his head and never looked our way and I watched him walk all the way out before thanking Sammy once again and slipped out of Cypress Grove myself.

Didn't have to worry about Father Callan. He didn't know Alizée's name or where she lived or worked. I planned to keep it that way. With her father gone, there was no way they could follow Mr. D to my building either. My only fear was they had done so before he left, maybe even discovered something about Alizée, before I put Mr. D aboard *SS Maraba*.

I checked with Kirk Eckland when he went to roll call at four p.m. Nothing.

I OFFERED TO bring my report to Audubon Place, but Angél rather pick it up herself, so I put the report in a manila folder at the edge of my desk, in front of one of the chairs and went behind to sit in my captain's chair, read the morning paper and drank my third cup of coffee-and-chicory.

Front page headline read: MacArthur Receives Triumphal Welcome.

A picture of a ticker-tape parade for the general in New York was accompanied by a story of his speech to Congress where he proclaimed, "… old soldiers never die, they just fade away." The man added, "And like the old soldier of the ballad, I now close my military career and just fade away, an old soldier who tried to do his duty as God gave him the light to see that duty."

Eloquent. Caesar was eloquent too and Robert E. Lee and soldiers like me have been leaving blood on the ground for centuries.

Eloquent?

Eloquent was the sergeant in the first world war, who jumped out of the trench to lead the charge that broke the German line at Belleau Wood He urged his fellow US Marines, "Come on, you sons of bitches. Do you want to live forever?"

Eloquent was the army ranger hunkered down on that bloody beach at Anzio with long-range German artillery raining hellfire down on us, the soldier next to me who shouted, "Pray! Pray to God for help!" He grabbed my arm. "But tell him not to send Jesus. This is no place for kids!"

I flipped to the sports page and my Yankees were 2-0 in the regular season, beating the Red Sox twice already. First game went 5-0 Yankees, the second 6-1 Yankees. Good start. Love beating those bean-towners.

Mr. I-don't-get-along-with-cats must have parked around the corner because Angél tapped on my office door and stepped in wearing a silver swing dress appropriate for dancing, silk, with a straight neckline and spaghetti straps with a sash belt and black high heels. Saw a picture of that same dress in yesterday's fashion page. Her face looked as if she'd just come from the D. H. Holmes cosmetic counter where professional make-up artists turned housewives into movie stars. Well, movie star lookalikes.

Whoever taught her to walk sensuously did not succeed.

"Hello Angél. Where are you singing tonight?"

"Singing?" She moved up slowly and sat in the chair on the right in front of my desk.

I pointed to the folder in front of her and she picked it up and read it. The ceiling fans brought her perfume over and it was nice, whatever it was.

How many times have I said many women look better at a distance? Angél looked better close up. She must have taken one of those speed-reading courses because she finished my piece of fiction pretty damn quickly.

"So, the man in jail actually did it."

"Yes"

"You sure?"

"I read his confession. There are things in it only the killer could possibly know."

"What things?" She reached up to run fingers through her brunette, June Allyson hairdo.

"If I tell you, then you'll know it too and it's a secret the police insist on keeping in case people like you make trouble. You're going to have to trust me on this."

"They let you see it."

"I'm almost one of them. I've actually helped on a few murders and I promised I wouldn't tell what I read. And I keep my word."

"So my father's mistress wasn't involved."

"Nope."

"Damn." She stuck out her lower lip. It's a lot cuter when Jeannie does it. "Do I owe you any money?"

"Nope." For some reason I don't think she liked me using 'Nope'.

"Oh, well. Time to move on." She stood. "Like my dress?"

"Yep."

"Well, I've decided I want a real boyfriend. A man. I'm tired of going out with boys."

"Sounds like good plan."

Wish she would just leave. I kicked my feet up on the desk. Maybe she'll get the hint.

Those brown eyes bored into mine. Dark, but not as dark as Alizée's, or as pretty.

She kept staring then slowly ran her tongue across her lips, wetting her lipstick.

"I've decided I want you to be my boyfriend."

I almost fell out of my chair pulling my legs down.

"I already have a girlfriend."

"She cannot be as rich and pretty as me. Well, not as rich for sure. Don't you think I'm pretty?"

"Of course, but I'm already involved."

Hold Me, Babe

She opened her purse, dug in and pulled out a narrow envelope. "I have tickets for us. Tomorrow. Frank Sinatra at the Blue Room."

"Angél, put your tickets away. You're not my type."

She slid the tickets away, put a hand on her hip. "What's your type?"

Jesus, why doesn't she just leave?

"Sultry. Like a gypsy."

"That's ridiculous. Do you know how wealthy I am?"

I started to get up, give her another hint but the door opened and Alizée breezed in, smiling at me. She wore a white blouse tied at the waist and blue jeans she'd cut into shorts that were too short. She was barefoot, hair in a ponytail. "You have to hear what Harri just did."

I sat back and introduced the two. Alizée kept walking, nodded to Angél and there was some feline-looking eye contact and I knew exactly what Alizée was up to. She came around the desk and I reached a hand out to her. She kept coming and turned and ended up sitting in my lap.

"Miss Brienne asked me to be her boyfriend."

"What did you tell her?"

"I told her she wasn't my type."

Alizée looked at me. "What is your type, anyway?"

"Sultry. Like a gypsy."

She took in a deep breath, those breasts within easy kissing range. She tapped my nose with a finger. "He says that because I'm as gypsy as it gets around here."

Angél waited for me to look at her.

"What is she, a teen-ager?"

"Missy," said Alizée. "I'm more of woman than you'll ever be."

Angél left a vapor trail. She also left her report.

Alizée tapped my nose again. "Who was that?"

"Former client."

"Was she serious about going out with you?"

I leaned forward to kiss her lips but she pulled back, smiling.

"Happens all the time," I said. "Women have been jumping on the hood of my car for years, hiring me to guard their bodies. You name it." I raised my left arm, made a muscle. "They all want a piece of this."

She laughed.

Always a good sign.

"What was that about Harri?"

She laughed louder. "I made that up."

SHE QUIT TELLING me I didn't have to go in with her. Alizée unlocked the door of the Varenne Building. I stood close enough to smell her Caliari. She wore a nice work dress, dark blue and fitted and not too long, her hair pinned up on the sides with barrettes. I wore my light gray suit, my .45 in a black holster on my right hip, an extra clip in my coat pocket. Just in case.

She flipped on the light next to the door, which was usually on and I felt the hairs stand on the back of my neck and spotted a slash of red on the hardwood floor to our right. Blood. I grabbed Alizée with my left hand and pulled her back, drawing my .45 and the explosion of gunfire reverberated in the small room and I yanked her down with me.

Three shots and heavy footsteps ran down the left hall.

I checked Alizée and she wasn't hit. Me either. I kicked the front door back open and kept a hold of her arm to go back out to the street. The door hit me in the face and sent me against Alizée and I saw a blue steel handgun. I yanked the door shut and shoved Alizée to the right. We crawled to the hall as four shots came through the door.

We scrambled to Alizée's office. She went in first and I closed and locked the door. There were two doors leading out of the place and I pointed to the phone.

"Call the police."

I locked the other doors from the inside, backed next to her to cover the doors as she told the operator to send the police. Bullets shattered the lock on the hall door and I pulled Alizée down behind the desk, took aim and bullets came through the door to our right. My heart slammed in my chest and I tried looking at both doors, keeping the .45 close to my chest, Ranger style, able to quickly point and shoot.

A shout and they came at the same time, firing and crashing through the doors. I hid behind the desk, felt bullets hitting it and I aimed at the man coming through the side door. He swung his pistol around, firing wildly and I squeezed one, two, three rounds, saw them hit him but the son-of-bitch wouldn't go down. Who doesn't go down when hit by a .45? He saw me and tried to aim at me and I fired four more rounds and saw his head snap back, knew I'd made a head-shot and he crashed against the desk and fell straight down.

I ejected my magazine and put the second one in. I was back to eight rounds now and the room was filled with the smell of gunpowder and blood. Alizée was under the desk, the doorway empty.

"You OK?"

She nodded, her eyes wide.

I peeked around the desk but the other man must have gone back into the hall.

"Did the operator get the address?"

Alizée shook her head. The phone lay in pieces next to us. A direct hit. Hell, someone on the street should have heard the gunfire, especially at the front door. I tried to catch my breath, calm down. She was breathing heavy too.

We could just wait him out, only I didn't like the positioning. He had three ways in and knew we were behind the desk now. I wiped sweat from my brow, motioned for her to stay put and eased around the side of the desk, squeezing past the dead man whose brains lay splattered against the wall. From this position, the desk blocked the door behind me now and I could cover the hall door and the door the dead man came through. Looked like another office in there.

I bolted for it, slid in and swung my .45 around. Empty. I came back into the doorway and whispered for Alizée. She peeked and I nodded for her to come my way. I had the office covered. She started to get up and I waved her down.

"Crawl."

She crawled over the dead man, right to me and we went into the next office, moving low, all the way to another door that led to a rear kitchen and I wondered what if there were more than two of them. I got a look at the dead man's face and it wasn't Joseph Darnand.

Damn. Where the hell were the police?

I knew the building was thick-walled but, Fuck.

A voice shouted from the hall, in French, sounding enraged. I looked at Alizée, who nodded. "He said give me to him. Called you a whore and a pig."

I'd caught the word *cochon*.

There was no back door to the kitchen that went outside, as I'd hoped. The rear door went back into the hall. There was a heavy wooden island with a stove in the center of the room and I positioned Alizée behind it, crouched, with me behind it as well and covering both doors as best I could with a weapon large enough to stop a charging rhino. Well, maybe not a rhino but eight bullets from a .45 should stop a man, long as I didn't miss.

The seconds ticked by and the thundering of my heartbeat lessened in my ears. Couldn't take a second to look down at Alizée, so I eased my knee over and touched her. She wrapped an arm around my calf.

The big man came in screaming, a pistol in each hand, throwing bullets and I leveled my weapon and fired and fired again and again, saw rounds strike the big bastard but he kept coming. He leaped and I fired and the bolt stayed back. I was out of ammo and the man fell over the island atop me and we crashed against the counter and went down.

What the fuck kind of maniacs were these guys?

I rolled him off me and he flopped on his back. My right arm burned and I saw a tear in my jacket when I checked his vitals. Nothing. Dead. Good. Only I was out of ammo. I picked up the pistol next to his hand, opened the cylinder. A .38 Smith and Wesson with six spent casings.

I felt Alizée's hand on my back.

"Stay down." I shoved my .45 back in the holster and went around on all fours to find the other pistol. Also a .38 S&W, also empty. American pistols. I took it back and searched the bastard's pockets, found loose rounds and loaded both pistols, sticking one in my belt, holding the other.

The man's face was turned away, so I moved it. Joseph Darnand.

"The Varennes," Alizée whispered and I nodded.

"Stay with me." No way I was leaving her anywhere.

I took her hand with my left, holding up the .38 and we kept low, moved around the island for the hall, peeked out.

We found Joseph Varenne unconscious behind his desk. He had a bloody bump on his head but was breathing OK. His brother was conscious, hiding in a closet with a bloody mouth. I moved back out to his desk and called the police.

"You're bleeding." Alizée touched my right shoulder.

I looked down at my right arm and it was throbbing now, so she worked my torn jacket off and helped pull my sleeve up. Wasn't a gunshot wound. Something gouged the shit out of my arm. She got a pair of scissors from the nearest desk and cut my shirt sleeve, wrapping a piece of it to shut off the bleeding. It was then I noticed blood on the front sights of the .38 in my hand, as well as some skin. My blood and skin, I'm sure. Son-of-a-bitch.

Alizée took in a deep breath and hugged me and I hugged her back.

"Dammit. You lost a barrette."

I wasn't sure if she was crying or laughing.

A minute later we went back to check on Joseph and the police finally arrived.

MY UNDERWOOD TYPEWRITER got a good, hard workout with Alizée typing my statement for the police after my arm was patched up. Frenchy had taken cursory notes at the scene, and took my .45 and the other guns, told me he'd be by later to pick up one of my Lucien Caye special statements.

"What did he mean by that?" Alizée had asked.

"I tend to get creative. I should write short stories."

Her hair hung loose and was messed up. She'd removed the other barrette. John Stanford sat in one of the chairs in front of my desk. He showed me his Webley .38 before he slipped it into the right front pocket of his brown smoking jacket. I had already retrieved my .357 magnum from the nightstand next to my bed.

Jeannie sat with Harri in the other chair in front of my desk. My daughter's eyes were red and Harri squirmed to be let down.

"I'm OK," I told her again and she nodded but didn't look convinced. I should put a shirt on to cover the bandage, even though Alizée said I looked pretty good in my undershirt.

I stood behind Alizée and dictated the final sentences of our collective statement, "Miss Diluviennes and PI Caye remained with Joseph Varenne until the police arrived and summoned medical assistance. Ambulance attendants brought the Varenne brothers and PI Caye to Charity Hospital where they were treated, Joseph Varenne suffering a contusion of the head and a concussion, Craig Varenne suffering a bloody lip and broken tooth, while six stitches patched up PI Caye's right arm."

She looked over her shoulder at me.

"Put 'End of Statement' and type two lines for us to sign and date."

As she did, Alizée said, "I don't see what's so special about your statement. It was just the facts."

"Police statement don't usual start 'On a balmy, spring morning' or describe men as 'villains, fiends and bastards'."

Jeannie put Harri up on the desk, came around and hugged me again.

"I'm OK, Sweetie. Really." She looked up at me, her lower lip quivering, so I told her, "The entire German army couldn't kill me during the war. What chance do you think two French thugs had?"

Maybe I shouldn't have let her hear the entire statement, knowing her father killed two men today, but this was the real world and she needed to know it wasn't all Wonderland. When she first came to me, she wasn't emotional at all. I took it for an inner strength. A kid dropped by her mother at a stranger's doorstep had to toughen her. It wasn't until later, when I caught her crying in bed one night, that we had our first long talk about her life.

Her mother didn't abuse her or anything like that and Ralph never touched her, only Jeannie said her mother rarely hugged or kissed her. I did.

Alizée signed and dated the statement and I reached around Jeannie to sign it as the phone rang. Alizée answered, "Lucien Caye, Private Eye." She winked at me.

"I know I'm not Pretty Baby," she said. "I'm prettier."

"Let me." Jeannie reached for the phone.

"It's – "

"I know who it is." Jeannie put a hand on the receiver and Alizée let go. My daughter put the receiver next to her face. "Mr. Frenchy? My Daddy's not pretty. He's handsome." She handed the phone back to Alizée and I heard Frenchy laughing.

I reached for the phone but Alizée told the lieutenant, "OK," and hung up.

"He'll come by for the statement in the morning."

Harri tried to leap from the desk all the way to the bookshelves, missed and fell to the floor, on her feet at least. Jeannie picked her up.

"OK, everyone. Supper's on Lucien Caye, Private Eye."

It took a while to reach an agreement. Po-boys. John said he'd stand guard and Jeannie reminded everyone. *Captain Video and his Video Rangers* was coming on.

FRENCHY CAPDEVILLE BREEZED in at nine a.m., stopped when he saw Alizée sitting behind my desk. She was in my robe.

"Right here," I said from the kitchen where I was fixing coffee.

He was surprisingly cigarette-less, waved to me and went to sit in a chair in front of my desk. Alizée brought our statement around, the bottom of my robe opening to show her legs. She handed him the statement and sat in the other chair, closing the bottom of the robe that had opened again to show her thighs.

I fixed three coffees, all with cream and sugar – pet milk actually. Alizée took one sugar, I took two and Frenchy three, as I recalled. It was my special extra strong coffee-and-chicory. I went and sat behind my desk.

Still looking at the statement, Frenchy said, "We're not releasing your names to the press. They've already assumed the Varenne brothers took out the bad guys and we all love to see how the newspapers can turn fact into fiction better than a science-fiction writer."

"Good. In case the fuckin' Unione Corse are still looking for Mr. D –"

Frenchy turned to Alizée. "Not anymore. I hate to be the one to tell you." He stared at her, let her figure what was coming.

"My Papa's dead, isn't he?"

Frenchy pulled out a telex. "From our friends in the Sureté. Copy of an AP teletype for *le Monde*. Paris newspaper. He showed it to her then me. The teletype was in French with an English translation below. It was titled 'War Hero Dies at Sea'."

He handed it to Alizée, who wiped her eyes and asked him to read it aloud.

"French Governor of Martinique, Joseph Le Lorrain, reports the captain of *SS Maraba* confirmed the death at sea of André Louis Diluviennes. M. Diluviennes, a former famous circus clown, fought with *le Maquis* during the war and was awarded the *Medal of the Resistance* and named a *Chevalier de la Légion d'Honneur* for his leadership role in the resistance during the liberation of Paris, 24-25 August 1944."

He looked at Alizée, who said, "*Chevalier* is a knight. My Papa was awarded the Legion of Honor." She put her hand to her throat and I knew she was touching the necklace her Papa gave her. I hadn't seen her without it since.

Frenchy went back to the article. "André Diluviennes was linked to the secret American-financed assassination group known as," Frenchy spelled out, "*Les anges de mort.*"

Alizée interpreted, "The Death Angels."

Never heard of them.

Frenchy went back to the article. "The war hero's body will be interred in the World War II Veterans Mausoleum in Marigot Cemetery, Fort-de-France, Martinique."

Alizée had her eyes closed now. Frenchy put the telex on the desk in front of her.

"Let's hope the Goddamn Unione Corse reads Parisian newspapers."

"It's an AP wire story. Should be reprinted all over the place."

"I wonder how the hell he got mixed up with the Unione Corse?"

Frenchy fought off a yawn. "Up early for the post-mortem. We're sending their fingerprints to the Sureté but the one you killed in the kitchen is probably Joseph Darnand. You shot him seven times, four wounds were fatal." He grinned at me. "Killed him four times. The other guy only had four wounds, two fatal."

Which meant I'd missed the first guy with three shots and one shot missing in the kitchen.

"Can't believe I missed at that range."

Frenchy's eyes lit up and I saw Alizée watching now.

"Moving targets *shooting at you*. Hell, they didn't get you or beautiful here – not once."

I looked at Alizée. *All it takes is once. Damn.*

Frenchy finished his coffee and left. Alizée sat there, staring at the bookcase. I finished my coffee and took my mug and Frenchy's to the sink. Alizée pulled her knees up and my robe fell off her legs. She reached a hand for me and I took it.

"It's hard to believe about my Papa."

I decided to get her out of the funk, if I could.

"I like those panties." They were white and sheer enough for me to make out her bush.

She looked down and laughed.

"It was only a matter of time when you'd see them." She reached both hands up and I leaned down and kissed her. The door opened behind us and I turned to see Edward Courant step in.

"Good. Both of you. That saves me a trip." He wore a black mortician's suit with a black tie, his hair even more frizzed out from the wind outside. I stepped away from Alizée who drew her knees down and closed the front of the robe. Courant stepped up, put his briefcase on the desk. I went around to my captain's chair.

The lawyer pulled out three manila folders and put them on the desk, then sat.

"Three new cases for you, Mr. Caye. There are case notes and three separate $500 retainer checks for you. Find these people, sir. Music people. One might be in Bay Saint Louis." He looked at Alizée. "As for you, Miss Diluviennes. I've excellent news. Lena Horne's version of *How Could You Leave Me* is number two on the blues charts. Each time a record is pressed you collect a royalty. The performance royalties as it's played on the radio will start coming in soon." He smiled at her then at me and then back to her.

"But there's better news."

Alizée waited. He held still a moment.

"Lena Horne just signed a contract to record your *Walk in the Moonlight* and there's interest from two other managers. Patti Page and Dinah Shore want to record your songs." He rubbed his hands together. "I told you I had contacts."

"Wow," she said.

"But contacts are no good without your talent. Please tell me you're working on more songs."

"I am."

He held out his hands. "Give me your hands."

She did and he stood and drew her to stand up.

"The fat man wants to meet you."

"I thought he was dead," I said.

"Huh? What?" Courant did a little dance, looked at Alizée once again. "Fats Domino wants to meet the girl who wrote *Creole Lady*. He's gonna record it."

The old fool started to swing Alizée around and her bare feet patted and the bottom of her robe opened nicely. He swung her around again and let her go and she just kept going, into it now, smiling at me.

Courant noticed her panties, his eyes lighting up and he put a hand over his mouth.

"Sorry."

She laughed. "Nothing you two haven't seen before." She stopped twirling and the robe closed and she came and sat in my lap.

Courant smiled. "Good. Now I know where to find both of you." He snatched up his briefcase.

"I'll call as soon as I know dates and times and all that." He backed toward the door. "And as soon as the checks come in." He went out, stopped the door before it closed and peeked back in. "Keep writing."

AT SUPPER THAT evening Jeannie reminded me her last day of school was Friday.

"I'll be there."

"We'll be there," Alizée corrected me.

We were having pizza.

"Are you all right?" Jeannie asked Alizée who nodded, said it had been a helluva day. Especially what she'd learned about her Papa.

Jeannie kept watching her until Alizée told her about her Papa dying.

"Oh, no."

"He was dying for a long time. He's not suffering anymore."

My daughter looked at me.

"I still can't believe he was a war hero," Alizée said.

Jeannie blinked at me, then at her.

"My Daddy's a war hero too. He has a medal with a silver star and a medal with a purple heart."

I caught Jeannie's eye. "How do you know that?"

"I found them in your dresser drawer and Uncle John said they were for bravery and getting wounded."

She took a bite of pizza.

"You were looking through my stuff?"

"You look through my stuff."

"I'm your father. I outrank you."

"Huh?" Jeannie took a drink of root beer.

"Wounded?" said Alizée. "Is that how you got the scar on your arm?"

"When did you see the scar on my arm?" It was up near my shoulder.

She giggled. "Yesterday. You were in your undershirt."

"Oh, yeah."

Jeannie laughed.

"What's so funny?"

"You're a detective and didn't figure that out."

Oh my God. Two females. I haven't got a chance.

I went back to my pizza.

A minute later, a crash drew us to the living room where Harri was on the end table on the far side of the sofa looking down at the lamp on the floor.

I'd miscounted. Three females.

SUMMER MEANS NO school and Jeannie is in the park across the street with her new friends. Two boys and two girls, a brother-sister pair and cousins to throw in. Not sure what they're playing but there are three hula-hoops flying around. I watch them and feel a tightness in my throat, remembering those kids back in Italy, barefoot boys and little girls with torn dresses asking us for something to eat. They didn't beg, they just stuck out a shaking hand.

"Per favore, Signore Americano."

And we gave them everything we had to eat. Tough guy Rangers all choked up.

I wonder what would have happened to Jeannie when her mother dropped her off if my little girl had turned and walked away from the building. Would I have never known her?

Last night Alizée and I had our first adult date. Movie and dinner and sex. Last year's Academy Award Best Picture made a return engagement at the Orpheum Theatre right off Canal Street. I'd missed *Sunset Boulevard* the first time around and the story of love, lust, avarice, a gigolo, an aging movie star, a flat tire and a dead body in a swimming pool was irresistible. Always liked William Holden.

Jeannie spent the night at Kaye's and Alizée took over when we got home, asking for a beer, going to the bathroom to come out naked as I sat on the sofa with two cold beers on the coffee table. She stood in the doorway with my dark bedroom behind her and the bright light of the living room bathing her body. She put her hands up on either side of the door frame, her left knee bent slightly and my gaze moved from the haughty look on her beautiful face, down past those breasts, bigger than I'd anticipated but not huge, small nipples pointed in anticipation of what I was about to do with them. I traced her narrow waist down to the mat of pubic hair that looked redder than her dark red-brown hair. Never realized how long her legs were under those long skirts. She took her hands and put them behind her neck and slowly pushed up the back of her hair, her breasts rising.

"You gonna say something, or not?"

"I didn't realize you were Medusa."

"Medusa?"

"You just turned part of me to stone. An important part."

She laughed. Always a good sign.

I stood and took off my clothes. The blinds were open and if anyone was on the balcony of the building across the park, they would get a good show. She watched me move slowly to her, checking me out, her gaze lingering on my dick that was straight up, like a flag pole and hard as – stone. I moved to her and she pulled her hands down, left them by her side. Inching closer, I stopped just before our bodies touched and leaned my mouth down. Her lips met mine and a charge went through me. We French kissed and I reached down, cupped her ass and pulled her close, feeling the weight of her breasts against me, her bush against my leg.

I scooped her up and took her to my bed and we ripped off the covers and sheets and kissed and my hands roamed to her breasts and then down to her bush and back up again. I pulled my mouth from hers and slowed down, kissing my way down her throat to each breast, licking them, suckling those nipples, feeling her body rise, her breath coming hard now.

Her breasts were hot and soft and firm and I made love to them as my hand rubbed her belly, her soft, silky bush, slipped between her legs that she'd opened and I felt the heat of her pussy lips and touched them lightly and she cried out and I kissed my way down to her silky pubic hair and let my tongue take over.

Determined to send her through a climax, I licked and sucked and licked her clit again, sliding a finger inside. She cried out, she yanked my hair and I kept going. She bounced and bucked and I kept going. She told me, "Now. Now." And I kept going. She tried to pull me up but I just kept going until she let go of my ears and bucked against me and collapsed.

I rolled off the bed, donned a condom and moved between her legs. She looked down, watched me move my dick to her. She reached down and guided it to her pussy and I worked my way in, all the way in and stayed there a good half minute, hard and throbbing, until I started pumping and she cried out and told me to screw her.

"Oh, Babe. Oh, Babe. Oh, Babe."

She hung on to my shoulders and I kept moving in and out, working her, working harder and quicker, my balls slapping her ass and I pounded her, kept it up until I was on the edge and stopped.

"No. No. Don't stop."

Her gorgeous face smiled at me and I didn't stop until I came in hot spurts.

I got rid of the condom, brought a warm wash rag back for her, along with our beers and we drank them and made love a second time, longer, deeper.

We lay on our backs in bed after and I began to drift. The ceiling fan cooled the night breeze flowing through the open transoms, taking the heat from our glistening bodies and she curled against me and fell asleep. The light from the living room illuminated her pretty face. I watched her breathe easily, softly. I sure liked this girl. A lot.

My eyelids drew heavy and closed and I felt myself slipping away and thinking how much I liked that she was a cuddler. I'm not sure if it was a dream moving in or just my damn sense of humor that brought the memory of an old girlfriend, one who was not a cuddler. While the sex knocked me out, it energized her so much, she cleaned house. Seriously. I lay dead to the world after a good, long humping and I heard rattling. There she was, butt naked, cleaning my bedroom windows at three in the morning, rattling the venetian blinds.

"What are you doing?"

"I have all this energy."

She looked damn sexy standing there so I told her to come back to bed and I'll get rid of that energy. I wiped us both out and fell asleep only to hear the vacuum cleaner.

IN THE SPRING of 1951, I solved an old murder case, killed a couple scum-bags, learned a .45 wasn't a cannon and realized the women I'd known up until then were, well, like passing trains in the night. Or is it ships?

I drew closer to my daughter, learned a few lines of *Jabberwocky* – slimy toads and all and thankfully *Captain Video and his Video Rangers* took a break until autumn.

If you guessed the most important part was the woman I tracked down through a cemetery, you'd be right. Alizée Marie Diluviennes, all five feet six inches, auburn haired, dark brown eyes. I sure hope I don't mess this up. My track record isn't very good.

She is a woman to cherish. To caress. She put it best –

Our time, Babe
You and me and New Orleans
Hold me, Babe
Hold me, Babe

THE END
Hold Me, Babe

The following short story is lagniappe,

something extra.

It's the story of how Lucien Caye met

Kaye and Charley Rudabaugh.

Hold Me, Babe

"The Heart Has Reasons"

a short story by O'Neil De Noux

First published in Alfred Hitchcock Mystery Magazine

Winner of the 2007 **Shamus Award** for **Best Short Story** by the Private Eye Writers of America.

FOR TWO DAYS she came and sat under the WPA shelter in Cabrini Playground with her baby, sometimes rocking the infant, sometimes walking between the oaks and magnolias, back and forth. Sometimes she would sing. She came around nine a.m. and around lunchtime she'd reach into the paper bag she'd brought and nibble on a sandwich. After, she would cover her shoulder with a small pink blanket and nurse her baby beneath the blanket. Around five p.m., she would walk away, up Dauphine Street.

On the third morning the rain swept in, one of those all-day New Orleans rainstorms that started suddenly then built into monsoon proportions. The newspaper said to expect showers brought in by an atypical autumn cool front from Canada, which would finally break the heat wave that has lingered through the sizzling summer of 1948. I grabbed two umbrellas and found her huddled under the shelter.

"Come on," I told her, "come get out of the rain." I held out an umbrella. When she didn't take it immediately, I stood it against the wall and stepped away to give her some room. She looked younger up close, nineteen, maybe eighteen and stood about five-two, a thin girl with short, dark brown hair and darker brown eyes, all saucered-wide and blinking at me with genuine fear.

I took another step away from her, not wanting to tower over her with my six foot frame, and smiled as warmly as I could. "Please. Come take your baby out of the rain." I opened the second umbrella and handed it to her.

Slowly, a shaky white hand extended for the umbrella, those big eyes still staring at me. I took a step toward the edge of the shelter. A loud thunderclap caused us both to jump and the baby started crying.

I led the way back across the small playground, the umbrellas pretty useless in the deluge, and hurried through the brick and wrought iron fence to narrow Barracks Street, having to pause a moment to let a yellow cab pass. She moved carefully behind me and I held the door to my building open for her. I closed the umbrellas and started up the stairs for my apartment. "I'll bring towels down," I called back to her, then took the stairs two at a time.

Moving quickly, I grabbed two large towels from my bathroom, lighting the gas heater while I was in there and pulled the big terry-cloth robe I never wore from the closet, draping it over the bathroom door before leaving my apartment door open on the way out. She stood next to the smoky glass door of my office, rocking her baby, who had stopped crying. She still gave me that frightened look when I came down and extended the towels to her.

"Top of the stairs, take a left. My apartment door's open." I reached into my suit coat pocket and pulled out a business card. "That's my office behind you. The number's on the card. Go upstairs. The heaters on in the bathroom and take your time. Lock yourself in. Call me if you need anything."

I shoved the towels at her and she took them with her free hand. I pressed the business card between her fingers as she moved away from my office door. She took a hesitant step

Hold Me, Babe

for the stairs, stopped and watched me with hooded eyes now.

Stepping to my office door, I told her, "I'm Lucien Caye," and nodded at my name stenciled on the smoky glass door. "I'm a detective."

Her lower lip quivered, so I tried my warmest smile again. "Go on upstairs. You'll be safe up there. Lock yourself in."

The baby began to whine. She took in a deep breath and backed toward the bottom step. Glancing up the stairs, she said, "First door on the left?"

"It's open," I said as stepped into my office. "I'll start up some eggs and bacon. I have a stove in here." I left the door open and returned to the row of windows along Barracks Street where I'd been watching her. A louder thunder clap shook the old building before two flashes of lightning danced over the rooftops of the French Quarter. The street was a mini-canal already, the storm washing the dust from old my gray, pre-war 1940 DeSoto coach parked against the curb.

"Bacon and eggs," I said aloud and turned back to the small kitchen area at the rear of my office. I had six eggs left in the small refrigerator, a half-slab of bacon and milk for the coffee. I sniffed the milk and it smelled OK.

I called my apartment before going up. She answered after the sixth ring with a hesitant, "Yes?"

"It's Lucien. Downstairs. I'm bringing up some bacon, eggs and coffee, OK?"

I heard her breathing.

"I'm the guy who got you outta the rain. Remember? Dark hair. Six feet tall. I brought an umbrella."

"The door's not locked," she said.

"OK. I'll be right up." When she didn't hang up immediately, I told her, "You can hang up now."

"All right." She did and I brought a heaping plate of breakfast and a mug of café-au-lait. I'd left my coat downstairs, along with my .38 revolver. Didn't want to spook her anymore than she was already spooked.

She was sitting on the sofa, her baby sleeping next to her. In the terry-cloth robe, a towel wrapped around her wet hair like a swami, she looked like a kid, not a mother. The baby lay on its belly, wrapped in a towel. I went to my Formica kitchen table and put the food down, flipping on the light and telling her I'd be downstairs if she needed anything else.

"Is that a holster?" she asked, staring at my right hip.

"I told you I'm a detective." I kept moving toward the door, giving her a wide berth, hoping the fear in her eyes would subside.

"Thank you," she said, standing up, arms folded across her chest now.

I pointed down the hall beyond my bathroom. "There's a washer back there for your clothes and a clothesline out back, if it ever stops raining."

She nodded and said, "I'm Kaye Bishop." She looked down at her baby. "This is Donna."

I stopped just inside the door. "Nice to meet you Kaye. If you need to call anyone, you know where the phone is."

I hesitated in case she wanted to keep talking and she surprised me with, "You're not how I would picture a detective."

"How's that?"

Her eyes, like chocolate agates, stared back at me. "You seem polite. Maybe too polite."

"You've been out there for three days. You all right?"

"We'll be fine when Charley comes for us."

"Charley?"

"Charley Rudabaugh. Donna's father. We're not married, yet. That's why I'm staying with the Ursulines."

Nuns. The Ursuline convent on Chartres Street. Oldest building in the Quarter. Only building which didn't burn in the two fires that engulfed the city in the Eighteenth Century, or so the story goes. For an instant I saw Kaye Bishop in a colonial costume, as a casket girl, labeled because they'd arrived in New Orleans with all their belongings in a single case that looked like a casket. Imported wives from France, daughters of impoverished families sent to the new world to marry the French settlers. The Ursulines took them under wing to make sure they were properly married before taken off by the early, rough settlers. Looks like they're still taking care of young girls.

"The church took us in." Her eyes were wet now. "We're waiting until Charley can get us a place."

Donna let out a little cry and Kaye scooped up her baby and moved to my mother's old rocking chair next to the French doors that opened to the wrought iron balcony wrapping around my building, along the second floor. As she rocked her baby, she reached up and unwrapped the towel on her head, shook out her hair and rubbed the towel through her hair.

The baby giggled and she giggled back. "You like that?" She shook her hair out again and the baby laughed. Turning to me, she said, "Can you get my purse? It's in the bathroom."

I brought it to her and she took out a brush and brushed out her short brown hair. Donna peeked up and me, hands swing in small circles, legs kicking.

"She's a beautiful baby," I said backing away, not wanting to crowd them.

Kaye smiled at her daughter as she brushed her hair, the rocker moving now. I was about to ask if the eggs and bacon were OK when she started humming, then singing in a low voice, a song in French, a song that sat me down on my sofa.

My mother sang that song to me. I recognized the refrain ... "l̲e *coeur a ses raisons que la raison ne connait point.*" Still don't know what it means. I wanted to ask Kaye but didn't want to interrupt her as she hummed part of the song and sang part.

I closed my eyes and listened. It was hard because I could hear my heart beating in my ears. When the singing stopped and I opened my eyes, Kaye was staring at me and I could see she wasn't afraid of me anymore.

TWO HOURS LATER, I was about to call upstairs to suggest I go over and pick up Charley, bring him here when she called and said, "Could you get a message to Charley for me?"

"Sure."

"He's working at the Gulf station, Canal and Claiborne. He's a mechanic," she said with pride.

Slipping my blue suit coat back on, I looked out at the rain still falling on my DeSoto. It wasn't coming down as hard now but I took the umbrella anyway after I went back and slid my .38 back into its holster. I started to grab my tan fedora but left it on the coat rack. Hats just mess up my hair.

It took a good half hour to reach the station on a drive that normally took fifteen minutes. Every car in front of me drove so slowly, it was as if these people had never seen rain before in one of the wettest city in the country. I resisted leaning on my horn for an old man wearing a hat two sizes too large for his pin head, wondering why he couldn't get his Cadillac out of first gear.

Forked lightning danced in the sky, right over the tan bricks of Charity Hospital towering a few blocks behind the Gulf station as I pulled in. The station stood out bright-white in the rain, illuminated by its lights normally on only at night. I parked outside the middle bay with the word "tires" above the doorway. The other bays, marked "lubrication" and "batteries" were filled with jacked-up vehicles.

Leaving the umbrella in my DeSoto, I jogged into the open bay and came face up with a hulking man holding a tire iron.

"Hi, I'm looking for Charley Rudabaugh."

He lifted the tire iron and took a menacing step toward me. I stumbled back, turning to my right as I reached under my coat for my revolver.

"Sam!" a voice boomed behind the man and he stopped but kept leering at me with angry eyes.

I kept the .38 against my leg as I took another step back to the edge of the open bay doors so he'd have to take two steps to get to me. I'd have to run or shoot him. Neither choice was a good one. A second hulking man, even bigger, came around the man with the tire iron. Both wore dark green coveralls with the orange Gulf Oil logos over their hearts.

The bigger man growled, "Who the hell are you?"

"Kaye Bishop sent me with a message for Charley."

"Kaye? Where is she?" He took a step toward me and I showed him my Smith and Wesson, but didn't point it at him.

"I'm a private detective. You wanna tell me what's goin' on?"

"You got an ID?"

Don't remember ever seeing Bogart, as Sam Spade or Philip Marlowe, showing his ID to anyone, but I had to do it – a lot. I reached into my coat pocket with my left hand and opened my credentials pouch for him and asked, "Where's Charley?"

The bigger man looked hard at my ID. "I'm Malone," he said. "Charley works for me. Where's Kaye?"

"At my office." I slipped my creds back into my coat pocket.

Malone turned his face to the side and spoke to his buddy with the tire iron. "He's too skinny to work for Joe. And his nose ain't been broke. Yet."

The man with the tire iron backed away, leaning against the fender of a Ford with its rear jacked up.

"I told you where Kaye is. Where's Charley?" I re-holstered my revolver but kept my distance.

"Don't trust the bastard," said the man with the tire iron.

I could see, in both sets of eyes, there was no way they were telling me anything. Maybe they'd tell Kaye. I suggested we get her on the phone. I stayed in the garage as Malone called my apartment from the office area. When he signaled for me to come in and get the phone, the first hulk finally put the tire iron down.

"Kaye?"

"Charley's in the hospital," she said excitedly. "Can you bring me to him?"

"I'll be right there." I hung up and looked at Malone. "You wanna tell me what happened now?"

Charley Rudabaugh was a good kid, a hard worker, but he borrowed money from the wrong man. Malone learned that tidbit that very morning when a goon came by with a sawed-off baseball bat and broke Charley's right arm.

"I was under a Buick and couldn't get out before the goon got away."

"The 'Joe' you thought I was working for?"

"No. A goon works for Joe Grosetto."

Malone explained Grosetto was a local loan shark. I asked where I could locate this shark but neither knew for sure. Charley would.

KAYE AND DONNA were waiting for me in the foyer of my building. I brought them out to the DeSoto under the umbrella and drove straight to Charity Hospital, parking at an empty meter outside the emergency room.

Charley Rudabaugh was about five-ten, thin build with curly light brown hair and green eyes. He smiled at Kaye and kissed Donna and finally noticed me standing behind them. His right arm in a fresh cast, Charley blinked and said, "Who are you?"

I let Kaye explain as she held his left hand, bouncing a gurgling Donna cradled in her free arm. He looked at me suspiciously, sizing me up, giving me that look a male gives another when he just showed up with his woman. When Kaye finished, more nervous now, she asked Charley what happened to him.

He turned to her and his eyes softened. He took in a deep breath and said, "Haney." She became pale and I pulled a chair over for her to sit, then went back to the doorway.

"He didn't ask where I was?" asked Kaye.

Charley shook his head. "He just wanted the money."

Kaye's eyes teared up and she pressed her face against his left arm and cried. Charley's eyes filled too and he closed them but the tears leaked out, down his lean face. Donna's arms swung around in circles as she lay cradled and I waited until one of the adults looked at me.

It was Charley and I asked, "How much money are we talking about?"

"This doesn't concern you."

Kaye stopped crying now and wiped her face on the sheet before sitting up.

I tried a different tack. "What school didya' go to?" The old New Orleans handshake. This was no public school kid. He told me he went to Jesuit. I told him I went to Holy Cross. Two Catholic school boys who'd gone to rival schools.

"Your parents can't help?" I asked. Jesuit was expensive.

"They don't live here anymore. And don't even ask about Kaye's parents. This is our problem."

"Everyone needs help, sometimes."

"That's what you do? Some kinda guardian angel?"

I shook my head, thought about it a second and said, "Actually, it's what I do most of the time. Help people figure things out."

"We can't afford a private-eye."

I tried still another tack. "How do I find this Grosetto? This Haney?"

Charley shook his head. Kaye wouldn't meet my eyes so I left them alone, went out in to the waiting area. Ten minutes later a blond-headed doctor went in, then a nurse. I caught the doctor on the way out. It was a simple fracture of both bones, the radius and ulna between wrist and elbow.

"It was a blunt instrument, officer," the doctor said. "Says he fell but something struck that arm."

I thanked the doc without correcting him that I wasn't a cop. The nurse was obviously finishing up, telling them how Charley had to move on soon as the cast was hard. Kaye turned her red eyes to me and I took in a deep breath. "I'll take you to the Ursulines, OK?"

Her shoulders sank. I turned to Charley. "So where have you been staying?"

"He's been sleeping at the Gulf station," Kaye said.

He shot her a worried look.

"They don't know," Kaye added. "He stays late to lock up and sleeps inside, opens in the morning."

I put my proposition to them to use my apartment and stepped out for them to discuss it, gave them another ten minutes before walking back in. Kaye shot me a nervous smile, holding Donna up now, the baby smiling too as her mother jiggled her.

I looked at Charley who asked, "I just wanna know why you're doing this."

"How old are you, Charley?"

"Twenty. And Kaye's eighteen. We're both adults now."

I nodded slowly and said, "I watched a young mother and her baby spend three days in that playground, avoiding the kids when they came, keeping to themselves until the rain blew in. I've got two apartments, one converted into an office downstairs with a sofa bed, kitchen and bath. I've slept down there before. You got a better offer?"

CHARLEY AND KAYE wouldn't volunteer any information about Grosetto and Haney and there was no way Malone and his tire-iron friend were going to be much help. But I knew who would. He was in too, sitting behind his worn government-issue gray metal desk, in a government-issue gray desk chair in an small office with gray walls lined with mug shots, wanted posters and an electric clock that surprisingly had the correct time.

Detective Eddie Sullivan had lost more of his red hair, making up for it with an old-fashioned handle-bar moustache. Grinning at me as I stepped up to his desk, he said, "I was about to get a bite."

"Me too."

So I bought him lunch around the corner from the First Precinct house on South Saratoga Street at Jilly's Grill.

Hamburgers, French fries, coffee and a wedge of apple pie for my large friend. Sullivan was my height exactly but outweighed me by a hundred pounds, mostly flab.

Eddie Sullivan was the Bunco Squad for the First Precinct, since his partner retired, without a replacement in sight. He handled con artists, forgers, loan sharks and the pawn shop detail, checking lists of pawned items against the master list of stolen articles reported to police. I waited until he'd wolfed down his burger and fries and was starting in on his slab of pie before bringing up Grosetto and Haney. He nodded and told me he knew both.

"Grosetto's a typical Guinea, short, olive-skinned, pencil thin moustache, weighs about a hundred pounds soaking wet. Haney is black Irish, big, goofy-looking. Typical bully." He stuffed another chunk of pie into his mouth.

"Grosetto? He mobbed up?"

Sullivan shook his head. "He wishes but he ain't Sicilian. I think he's Napolitano or just some ordinary Wop. You got someone willin' to file charges against these bums?

"Maybe. I need to know where they hang out."

"Easy. Rooms above the Blue Gym. Canal and Galvez."

I knew the place and hurried to finish my meal as Sullivan ordered a second wedge of pie. He managed to say, between mouthfuls, "I'd go with you but I gotta be in court a one o'clock. Drop me by the court house?"

As he climbed out of my DeSoto in front of the hulking, gray Criminal Courts Building, Tulane and Broad Avenues, he thanked me for lunch, adding, "See if you can talk your friend into pressing charges. I could use a good collar."

"I'll try."

THE BLUE GYM was hard to miss, sitting on the downtown side of Canal and Galvez Streets. Painted bright blue, it stood three stories, the bottom two stories an open gym with six boxing rings inside, smelling of sweat, blood and cigar smoke. I weaved my way through a haze of smoke to a back stairs and went up to a narrow hall that smelled like cooked fish. A thin man in boxing shorts came rushing out of a door and almost bumped into me.

"Oh, 'scuse me," he said.

"I'm looking for Grosetto."

He pointed to the door he'd just exited and rushed off. I reached back and unsnapped the trigger guard on the holster of my Smith and Wesson before stepping through the open door to spot a smallish man behind a beat-up wooden desk. The man glared at me with hard brown eyes, trying to look tough, hard to do when he stood up and topped off at maybe five-three and skinny as a stick-man. He wore a shark-skin lime green suit.

"Who the hell are you?" he snarled from the right side of his tiny mouth.

I stepped up, keeping an eye on his hands in case he tried something stupid and said, "How much does Charley Rudabaugh owe you?"

"Huh?"

"How much?" I kept my voice even, without a hint of emotion.

The beady eyes examined me, up and down, then he sat and said, "You ain't Italian. What are you? Some kinda Mexican?"

I wasn't about to tell this jerk I'm half French, half Spanish, so I told him, "I'm the man with the money. You want your money, tell me how much Charley owes you."

"Three hundred and fifty. Tomorrow it's gonna be four hundred."

"I'll be right back." And I didn't look back as strolled out, making it to the nearest branch of the Whitney Bank before it closed. My bank accounts, I have a saving account now, were both in good shape after the Duponceau Case. As I stood in the teller line, I remembered the salient facts that brought such money into my possession –

It was a probate matter. When it got slow, I'd go over to civil court, pick up an inheritance case. This one was a search for any descendants of a recently deceased uptown matron. Flat fee for my work. If I found someone, they got the inheritance, if not, the state got it. I'd worked a dozen before and never found anyone until I found Peter Duponceau, a fellow WWII vet, in a VA Hospital in Providence, Rhode Island.

Not long after I caught a bullet from a Nazi sniper at Monte Cassino, he collected a chest full of shrapnel from a Japanese bombardment on a small island called Saipan. Peter was the grandson of the recently deceased uptown matron. His mother was also deceased. When I met him to confirm his inheritance, he was back in the hospital for yet another operation. At least the last months of his life were lived in luxury in an mansion overlooking Audubon Park. He left most of his estate to several local VFW chapters and ten percent to Lucien Caye, Esquire. When the certified check arrived, I contemplated getting an armored car to drive me to the bank. I couldn't make that much money in five years, unless I robbed a bank or two.

GROSETTO WAS BACK behind his desk but there was an addition to the room, a hulking man standing six-four, outweighing me by a good hundred pounds of what looked like grizzle, with a thick mane of unruly black hair and a ruddy complexion. He wore a rumpled brown suit as he stared at me with dull, brown eyes, Mississippi River water brown. My Irish friend Sullivan described Haney as black Irish, probably descended from the Spanish of the Great Armada, the ones who weren't drowned by the English. The ones who took the prevailing winds, beaching their ships along the Irish coast to be taken in by fellow Catholics to later breed with the locals. I would have given Haney only a cursory look, except I didn't expect he'd be so young, early twenties maybe.

Stepping up to the desk, I dropped the bank envelope in front of Grosetto. "Rudabaugh sign anything? Promissory note? IOU?" I knew better but asked anyway.

Grosetto picked up the envelope and counted the money, nodding when he was finished. I turned to Haney. "You still have that baseball bat?"

He looked at Grosetto for an answer and then looked back and I could see he wasn't all there.

"Try that stunt again and I'll put two in your head. And I'll get away with it."

"Alls I want is the girl," Haney said.

"What?"

He looked down at his feet, all shy-like and said, "I seen her," looking up now with those dull eyes, "*Real* pretty." He followed with a childlike chuckle.

I turned back to Grosetto, "Better let him in on the real world."

Grosetto was smiling now, or trying to with that crooked mouth. "He usually gets what he wants."

"Not this time," I said.

No use arguing with idiots. When I got back to my office, I located my black jack, a chunk of lead attached to a thick spring, covered with black leather, brand named the Bighorn because it allegedly could cold-cock a charging bighorn ram.

I only used it twice back when I was a patrolman and it worked well enough to incapacitate bigger, combative men. Then I put away my .38 and brought out my army-issue Colt .45 caliber automatic and loaded it, switching holsters now. I needed something with stopping power.

I called upstairs and Kaye answered, telling me the baby and Charley were asleep.

"I need to get a couple things, OK?"

She let me in and I quickly packed a suitcase with essentials, grabbed a couple suits and fresh shirts. Before stepping out, I waved her over and we whispered in the hall. I told her they owed Grosetto nothing. How? I told her someone had given me a lot of money and now I was giving them some.

"Charley won't stand for it. We'll pay you back."

I shrugged, then watched her eyes as I told her I'd met Haney. She blanched, so I followed it with, "Back at Charity, why did you ask Charley if Haney asked where you were?"

She took a step back, crossed her arms and said, "Haney's my half-brother."

SITTING AT MY desk in my dark office, I watched the rain finally taper off.

"What about your parents?" I'd asked Kaye up in the hall. She told me her father was dead and her mother had abandoned her when she was five and wouldn't say anything else about the matter, not even who'd raised her.

I was thinking – at least they were safe for now – just as I spotted Haney standing next to the playground fence across the street. Didn't take him long to find us. He stood there for a good ten minutes before coming across the street. I expected the baseball bat, not the revolver stuck in the waistband of his suit pants as he stepped in the foyer of my building. I'd moved into the shadows next to the stairs, black jack in my left hand. Slowly, I eased my right hand back to my .45 as he saw me and said softly, "Where is she?"

The sound of squealing tires behind him made him look over his shoulder. When he looked back I had my .45 pointed at his face and said, "That'll be the cavalry."

Two uniforms alighted from the black prowl car and came into the building with their guns out. It was Williams and Jeanfreau, both rookies when I was at the Third Precinct. I lowered my weapon. "He's got a gun in his waistband."

Williams snatched Haney's revolver and Jeanfreau cuffed him and dragged him out.

"Aggravated Assault, right?" Williams checked with me for the charge.

"Yeah. Hopefully he's a convicted felon." A felon with a firearm would hold Haney for a while.

"Thanks," I called out to my old compadres.

Williams called back, "Your call broke up the sergeant's poker game. But only for a while."

CHARLEY SAT SHIRTLESS at my kitchen table holding Donna with his good arm, Kaye in my terry cloth robe again, getting us coffee, them looking like a family now and I had to tell them about Haney. Kaye blanched at the news; Charley just nodded while Donna gurgled.

"How close are you?" I asked.

"I'm not even sure he's my half-brother," Kaye answered. "He claims to be. Claims my dad was his father. I never met him until he showed up at the hospital when Donna was born." She didn't volunteer any more and I didn't want to cross-examine her, sitting at my table, all three adults sipping coffee which wasn't bad and I'm picky about my coffee.

I turned to Charley and said, "We need to press charges against Grosetto. I'll back you and we'll put the slime-ball away. My buddy Detective Sullivan is chomping at the bit to nail him."

Charley shook his head and told me, in careful, low tones how he wanted Grosetto and Haney and all of it behind him, how he was going to pay me back whatever it cost me. I tried for the next half hour, but there was no changing his mind. He said he didn't want to be looking over his shoulder for the rest of his life. God, he was so young.

The coffee kept me up a little while, but the rain came back that night, slapping against my office windows as I lay on my sofa-bed. Why was I lying there? Why wasn't I out on the town, dancing with a long tall blonde in a slinky dress? Maybe bringing her here or going to her place and helping her slip into something more comfortable, like my arms.

I knew the answer. It was upstairs with those kids, so I lay waiting for trouble to return, knowing it would.

ARRIVING AT THE Criminal Courts Building early, I searched the docket for Haney's name, wanting to get a word in with the judge before his arraignment. When I couldn't find his name, the acid in my stomach churned. I snatched up a pay phone in the lobby and called parish prison, speaking to the shift lieutenant who took his time, but looked up the name for me.

"Haney. Yeah. Bonded out four-thirty a.m."

I asked more questions and got the obvious answers, a friendly judge and an friendlier bail bondsman had Haney out before sunrise. The only surprise was that Haney had only two previous arrests, both misdemeanors, no convictions.

I should have gotten a speeding ticket on the way home, but no one was paying attention. Catching my breath when I

Hold Me, Babe

reached the top of the stairs, I tapped lightly on the door. Even a bachelor knows better than to ring a doorbell with a baby inside. Kaye answered and I let out a relieved sigh, which disappeared immediately when she told me Charley wasn't there.

"Where'd he go?"

"To work. Malone picked him up." Her eyebrows furrowed when she saw the worried look in my eyes. I pointed to the phone and she opened the door wider, telling me, "Malone said a one-armed Charley was better than any of his other mechanics."

She knew the number by heart and I dialed. Malone answered after the fifth ring and I warned him about Haney being out of jail.

"Didn't know he was in jail."

"Well, he had a gun last night, so be on the lookout."

Then I called Sullivan to make sure the patrol boys did a drive-by at the Gulf Station before I went to see Grosetto.

HE WAS BEHIND the desk wearing the same lime green suit, sporting that same crooked slimy grin when I walked in on him, the place reeking of fish again.

"Where's Haney?"

Grosetto tried growling, which only made him look like a randy terrier, instead of a gangster. His hands dropped below the desk top and I turned my left shoulder to him, pulling out my .45, letting him get a look at it.

"Put your hands back on your desk and they better be empty."

"Who da' heller you comin' in here, tellin' me what to do?"

"Where's Haney?"

He tried smiling but it looked more like a grimace. "I'm glad you come by. You needa tell Charley he owes another fifty. I, how you put it, miscalculated the amount." This time it was a smile, sickly, showing off yellowed-teeth.

I shot his telephone, watched it bounce high, slam against the back wall, the loud report of my .45 echoing in my ears. Pointing it at his face now, I said. "Put your hands back on your desk."

He did, his eyes bulging now. I backed up and locked the door behind me and came back to the desk as I holstered my weapon, slammed both hands against the desk, shoving it across the linoleum floor with him and his chair behind, pinning him against the wall.

"Tell Haney I'm looking for him."

Three boxers and two trainers were in the narrow hall. I opened my coat and showed them the .45 and they backed away cautiously, none of them saying anything until I started through the gym. A couple brave ones cursed me behind my back, but kept their distance.

I FIGURED HANEY was loony enough to come by but it was Grosetto, just before midnight. He wore a gray dress shirt and black pants, hands high as he stepped into my building's foyer. I was sitting in darkness, half-way up the stairs, sitting in my shirt and pants with my .45 in my right hand.

"That you?" he called out when I told him to freeze. I'd unscrewed the hall light.

"What do you want?"

"I come to tell you somethin'."

I went and patted him down, closed and locked the building door then shoved him into my office, leaving the door open. He smelled like cigarette smoke and stale beer. I made him stand still as I moved to my desk and leaned against it.

"All right, what is it?"

"I made a mistake. Charley don't owe me nothin'."

"Good."

He tried smiling again, but it still didn't work. "I checked on you. You got some rep. You know. War hero. Ex-cop. Bad when you gotta be bad." He looked around my office for a second. "You check up on me?"

"In the dictionary. Under scum bag."

"You funny. You owe me a phone, you know."

Maybe it was the twitch in his eye or the way he sucked in a breath when I heard it, a thump upstairs. Grosetto should never play poker. It was in his eyes and I was on him in three long strides, slamming the .45 against his pointed head, tumbling him out of my way.

I took the stairs three at a time, reaching the top of the stairs as a gunshot rang out. My apartment door was open and a woman's screaming voice echoed as I ran in, scene registering as I swung my .45 toward the figure standing with a gun in hand. The gun turned toward me and I fired twice, Haney bouncing on his toes as the rounds punched his chest. The gun dropped and he fell straight back, head ricocheting off an end table.

Kaye, with Donna in her arms, moved for Charley as he lay on the kitchen floor, a circle of bright red blood under him. Holstering my weapon, I leaped toward them as Kaye cradled his head in her arms. He was conscious, a neat hole in his lower abdomen, blood oozing through his white undershirt. I jumped back to the phone and called for an ambulance. When I turned back, Charley was trying to sit up.

"Don't!" I jumped into the kitchen, snatched an ice tray from the freezer, broke up the ice, wrapped it in a dishcloth and got Kaye out of the way with Donna screeching now. I pressed the ice against the wound and told Charley to keep calm, the ambulance would be right there. Then I remembered I'd locked the foyer door and had to go down for it.

Charley was still conscious when they rolled him out with Kaye and Donna in tow. Williams and Jeanfreau had accompanied the ambulance and used my phone to call the detectives.

"What'd you shoot him with?" Williams asked, pointing to the two large holes around Haney's heart. I pointed to my .45 which I'd put on the kitchen counter before they came in.

It was then I remembered Grosetto and brought Williams down to my office. The little greaseball was just coming around and Williams slapped his cuffs on him and brought him up to have a look at Haney. The dead man looked younger in death in a yellow shirt and dungarees, his eyes even duller now, his face flaccid. To me he looked like an eighth grader trying to pass himself off at a high school. His shoes were tied in double knots as if his mom had made sure they wouldn't come undone.

It took the detectives forty minutes to get there. I made coffee for all and was on my second cup when Lieutenant Frenchy Capdeville strolled in, trailing cigarette smoke, a rookie dick at his heels. Frenchy needed a haircut badly, his black hair in loose curls over the collar of his brown suit.

His rookie partner had tried a pencil-thin moustache, like Frenchy's but his was lopsided. "Joe Sparks," Frenchy introduced him to me. Sparks, also in a brown suit, was sharp enough to keep quiet and let Frenchy run the show, which he did, quickly and efficiently.

After the coroner's men took Haney away, they took me and Grosetto to the Detective Bureau, Frenchy calling in

Eddie Sullivan. While they booked Grosetto, I gave a formal statement about the first man I'd shot since the war. Self-defense, defined in Louisiana's Napoleonic Code Law was – justifiable homicide.

IT DIDN'T TAKE a detective to discover how Haney had come in the back way, through the broken fence of the building next door, across the back courtyard and up the rear fire escape to break the hallway window.

"How'd he get in the apartment?" I asked Kaye as we sat in the hall at Charity Hospital the following morning, while Charley slept in the recovery ward. Dark circles around her eyes, she looked pale as she rocked Donna slowly. Thankfully the baby was asleep.

"I heard scratching against the door and thought it was the cat, the black one that's always around."

"Did he say anything?"

"No. He just shoved past me and shot Charley. Then he stood there looking at me."

A nurse came out of Charley's room and said, "He's awake now."

I didn't go in. I went back home to look up my landlord.

CHARLEY RUDABAUGH SPENT six days in the hospital. When I brought him home and walked him past my apartment door to the rear apartment, he balked until Kaye opened the door and smiled at him.

"What's going on?"

Kaye pulled him in and I stood in the doorway, amazed at what she'd done with the place in a few days. It came furnished but she'd brightened it up, replaced the dark curtains with yellow ones, the place looking spotless. Donna, lying on her back in a playpen in the center of the living room was trying to play with a rubber duck, slapping at it and gurgling.

It took Charley a good minute to take in the scene as Kaye eased up and hugged him.

"Here's the deal," I told them over coffee at their kitchen table. "The landlord gave us a break on the place. I'm fronting y'all the money. You don't have to pay me back, but if you insist, you can, but get on your feet first." I'd just put any money they gave me in a bank account for Donna's education.

Then I explained about how it really wasn't my money. It had been a gift and I was sharing it. "Everyone needs help sometimes. And you two have had a bad time recently."

I could see Charley was still confused, but not Kaye, beaming at him, paying little if any attention to me. I thanked her for the coffee and stood up to leave. Charley's eyes narrowed as he asked, "I understand what you say, but it's just hard to figure you ain't got some kinda motive. Everybody does."

I started for the door, turned and said, "Sometimes things are exactly as they appear to be."

Kaye moved to her daughter and began humming that same song, repeating the line in French again, "*le coeur a …*"

"What is that?" I had to ask.

"It's the reason you're doing all this." She smiled at me, looking like a school kid in her white shirt and jeans. "An old French saying that goes, 'The heart has reasons of which reason knows nothing'." She smiled down at her baby.

It wasn't until later, as I sat in my mother's rocker looking out the open French doors of my apartment, out at the dark roofs of the Quarter with the moon beaming overhead, that I heard my mother's voice back when she was young, a voice I haven't heard for so long, as she sang, *"le coeur a ..."*

Then it hit me.

The heart has reasons of which reason knows nothing. Kaye hadn't meant just me. It cut both ways. She'd also meant Haney and I felt the hair on the back of my neck standing up.

The End of
"The Heart Has Reasons"

Note from the publisher
BIG KISS PRODUCTIONS

If you found a typo or two in the book, please don't hold it against us. We are a small group of volunteers dedicated to presenting quality fiction from writers with genuine talent. We tried to make this book as perfect as possible, but we are human and make mistakes.

BIG KISS PRODUCTIONS and the author are proud to sell this book for as low a cost as possible. Good fiction should be affordable.

Also by the Author

Novels
Battle Kiss
Bourbon Street
Mafia Aphrodite
Mistik
Slick Time
USS Relentless
The French Detective
Death Angels

LaStanza Series Novels
1. *Grim Reaper*
2. *The Big Kiss*
3. *Blue Orleans*
4. *Crescent City Kills*
5. *The Big Show*
6. *New Orleans Homicide*
7. *The Blue Nude*
8. *The Long Cold*

Beau Series Novels
1. *John Raven Beau*
2. *City of Secrets*
3. *Nude in Red*

Caye Series Novels
1. *New Orleans Rapacious*
2. *Enamored*
3. *Hold Me, Babe*

Short Story Collections
LaStanza: New Orleans Police Stories
New Orleans Confidential
New Orleans Prime Evil
New Orleans Nocturnal
New Orleans Mysteries
New Orleans Irresistible
Hollow Point & The Mystery of Rochelle Marais
Backwash of the Milky Way

Screenplay
Waiting for Alaina

Non-Fiction
A Short Guide to Writing and Selling Fiction
Specific Intent

Hold Me, Babe

For more information about the author go to
http://www.oneildenoux.net

O'Neil De Noux would like to hear from you. If you liked this book or have ANY comment, email him at denoux3124@yahoo.com

If you enjoyed **HOLD ME, BABE** and would like to read more adventures of New Orleans Private Eye Lucien Caye you may want to check out other books in the series –

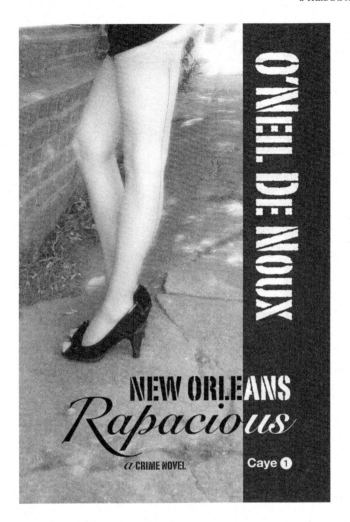

NEW ORLEANS RAPACIOUS

A wandering daughter case turns deadly in 1947 New Orleans as Lucien Caye searches for a strawberry-blond temptress with a curvaceous body and Prussian-blue eyes that blink ever so slowly, precisely, like a falcon and he realizes – rapacious, like a raptor, a bird of prey.

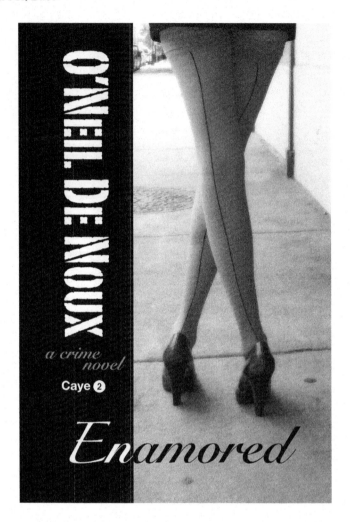

ENAMORED

A case of obsession and murder, a case that will baffle Lucien, intrigue him, make him fall in love – three times.

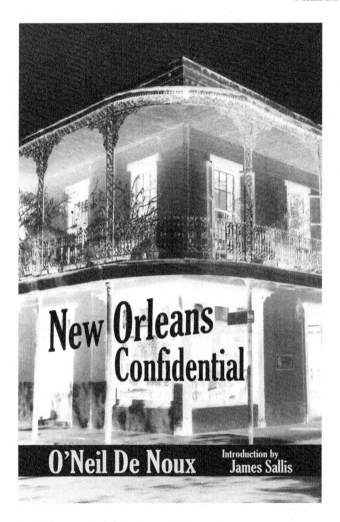

NEW ORLEANS CONFIDENTIAL

Eleven short stories. Come prowl the lonely, violent streets of American's most exotic city, the city that care forgot, New Orleans, with lone-wolf private eye Lucien Caye.

OTHER BOOKS by O'Neil De Noux
http://www.oneildenoux.net

O'Neil De Noux

The French Detective

A NOVEL OF
NEW ORLEANS
IN 1900

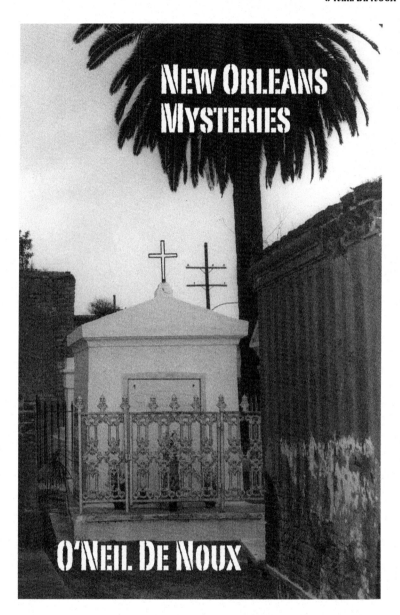

CPSIA information can be obtained
at www.ICGtesting.com
Printed in the USA
LVOW13s1540270717
542867LV00010B/625/P